i

MW01528150

The Masters Review

ten stories

Volume II

Jennifer Dupree · Andrew Patyon · Zoe Vandeveer
Courtney Gillette · Dustin M. Hoffman
Louise Ells · Jane Summer
Laurie Ann Cedilnik · Drew Krepp · Traci Cox

Stories Selected by A.M. Homes
Edited by Kim Winternheimer

Editor's Note

I'm so pleased to share with you our anthology, *The Masters Review*, with stories selected by A.M. Homes for its second volume.

The goal of The Masters Review is to showcase emerging authors, specifically those in graduate-level creative writing programs. Our feeling, after reviewing submissions from programs around the world, is that these authors represent unique, talented, and diverse voices. They are ten authors we believe will continue to produce great work.

Each year we pair with an established judge to select our stories from a shortlist compiled by our editorial team. Last year we worked with the wonderful and talented, Lauren Groff, who chose stories for a collection that was serious, heartfelt, and urgent. This year, recent Women's Prize for Fiction winner A.M. Homes, selected stories she calls, "compelling, startling, and resonant." In *Dancing at the Zoo* a young woman grapples with a car accident she witnessed as well as the lion living in her belly. *Potomac* by Andrew Payton was recently a finalist for The Chicago Tribune's Nelson Algren Award and addresses a brotherly conflict. In our narrative nonfiction essays, *How to Like Girls*, *Missed*, and *The Brackish*, our authors transform personal experience into a notion that can be appreciated by everyone, and in *Coffee for Dead Children*, the narrator worries that she and her boyfriend's "presence will be awkward, that people will think they're rubberneckers, that their very aliveness will be an affront to death." Each of our authors has something unique and special to offer, and I'm so pleased to be sharing their work with you.

Kim Winternheimer

The Masters Review

The Masters Review, Volume II.
Edited by Kim Winternheimer
Stories selected by AM Homes

Front cover photo: istock photo gallery

Interior Design by MG Book Design
www.mgbookdesign.com

First printing.

ISBN 978-0-9853407-1-1

Printed in the U.S.A.

Contents

Introduction

When young writers ask how can they tell if their work is good enough I tell them that it has to be compelling enough, finely enough wrought that it makes the reader want to stop what they're doing, to suspend living their life and enter the world the author has crafted for them.

These ten stories do that; they were written because they had to be, there is urgency to them, their authors are writers for whom silence is not an option.

These stories are about the stuff of life, birth, and death, and all that comes in between, brothers and sisters and parents—a lot about parents. They are about running away—both literally and emotionally, and they are about discovery, the unveiling of secrets, the revelation that comes with knowing oneself. They are stories which celebrate the power to illuminate, to document that which is historic, and to change what will happen in the future—i.e. they have the power to make a difference

There is nothing frivolous here, nothing done solely for entertainment, though they are certainly entertaining and artful and well crafted. More importantly, they are compelling, and more than compelling they are startling and terrifying and resonant.

My teacher, the writer, Grace Paley used to talk to us about writing, the truth according to the character, which means asking yourself, "Is this true for this person?" defining the space between author and character. That is one of the first things that someone who is going to be a writer must learn—that while the kernel of a story often comes from real life—the true story, the exploration of characters involved and the narrative action is the stuff of imagination.

Within these ten stories and surely in the narrative nonfiction pieces, there is a strong sense of personal experience, but these authors have moved from singular experience into communal one, into the journey that is one of making sense of what happens and why, and what it means to us and what we mean to each other.

As much as one can lose oneself in a story—one finds oneself as well. In these ten stories I found ten strong voices, ten writers I want to hear more from. I hope you enjoy reading them as much as I did.

A.M. Homes
New York City

The Masters Review
ten stories

Dancing at the Zoo

Jennifer Dupree
Stonecoast, MFA

If she could get rid of the full-up, furry feeling in her esophagus, Bonnie would like to complement the police officer on his posture. And she'd like to apologize for the dishes in her sink, and the fact that she never got around to putting any kind of lampshade over the light bulb, even though she looked at a whole variety of them at the Home Depot. But this police officer, like the ones she's seen on TV, seems interested only in the facts, and writing them down in his black and white notebook. Bonnie takes a sip of the milk she poured for herself just before he knocked and asked for a few minutes of her time. The lion inside her, which she understands to be the cause of her furry feeling, wanders through her bladder. Bonnie crosses her legs and bounces one foot on top of the other. The officer leans back against the edge of her sink and asks her to start at the beginning.

"People shouldn't be out like that, in the middle of the night. And he wasn't even wearing anything reflective, even though it looked like he was dressed to go jogging. Not that I'm saying it was his fault. But certainly he's old enough to know better. What did you say he was? Twenty? Twenty-two?"

The officer smiles with his May-colored eyes and Bonnie smiles back. His nametag says McDaid and she wonders if his hair, under his cap, is red. His eyebrows are brown with maybe a tint of red in them but it's hard to tell with the kitchen light like an ill-trained spotlight. She fingers the dry edge of her own cinnamon-colored hair. "It's not like I was snooping or anything. Anyone in my position could have heard them arguing like they were. My window was open." Bonnie presses her hands to her stomach to quiet the lion who is now pacing through her small intestine, giving her the sensation of socks in a mesh bag rolling around in the laundry. "I don't know about you," she says, feeling a little breathless from all the activity inside her, "But my mother always taught me to keep private things private."

Officer McDaid notes this in his little notebook and Bonnie imagines him bringing it out later, maybe showing it to his girlfriend or a colleague, and saying that it's as good a motto as any to live by. "You work at the newspaper, don't you?" He turns back a few pages.

This makes Bonnie wonder what else he has written down. "Just in advertising," she says. When she goes back to work, the journalist-people will sit on the edge of her desk, and tell her how nice she looks in her orange skirt, and bring her tea with lemon. And they'll pretend it's just casual, just conversation, and maybe they won't even write anything down. But Bonnie knows better and she'll listen for the whir of a tape recorder, even though some of those little ones are so quiet now. She'll have to tell them the car was blue, dark, maybe with a grayish tint to it and that the young man was tall but she couldn't say how tall, exactly, unless she was standing next to him, which she wasn't. And she'll tell them the woman was wearing a camel-colored coat and the airbag never went off. They won't like it but she'll insist that's all she has to say.

Bonnie feels a paw reach into her throat and give a little squeeze. She coughs into the sleeve of her bathrobe, leaving a wet mark the size of a kiss.

"Do you need some water?" Officer McDaid asks. Bonnie smiles and tells him what a good job his mother did raising him.

She first became aware of the lion inside her while she was standing outside on the sidewalk, watching the cops mark off where the car hit the young man. She was half-listening to Sheila Flint from next door give her account of what she heard and saw, and half-trying to hear what the cops were saying to each other. Sheila was saying she didn't hear a thing because her air conditioning had been running all night. "It wasn't even seventy degrees," Bonnie said, even though she knew she shouldn't be so judgey. And then, just while she was standing there about to ask Sheila if she actually *saw* anything, a lion's tail swished up into her throat, almost all the way to her nose. She clutched the silky fabric of her bathrobe at her collarbone and swallowed against the sudden and inappropriate urge to laugh. Sheila gave her an uppity look so Bonnie let go of her bathrobe, covered her face, and pretended to sob.

There was nothing funny about the scene out there—the young man with his head cracked open like a walnut on the tar, the skinny woman with her arms up over her massive blonde hair. The screaming, the wailing. Although Bonnie hadn't been able to make out most of what they said, she'd been listening to the woman and the young man go back and forth for a good five or ten minutes before anything else happened. She'd sat there on her bed, in front of her open window, and tried not to think about the things her parents used to yell at each other. She remembered her mother's face, streaked red and squinty-eyed and her father, with his lips like strung-tight fishing line. "It seemed like a lover's quarrel," she says to Officer McDaid, who taps his pencil on his notebook, lead side down, making little dots and dashes like a code of some kind. And then, because she feels bad about everything, "People sometimes say things they don't mean, you know."

"Did you hear something specific?"

Bonnie shakes her head. She probably could give him some specifics, if he pressed, but she doesn't want to seem like the kind of middle-aged woman who doesn't have enough of her own business to mind. She isn't just going to sit here at her kitchen table and gossip with this man she hardly knows as if they're the kind of best girlfriends you see in the movies. But if truth be told she heard words, and a few phrases, and certainly she saw the way the young man strutted toward the car and leaned into the window, so possessively you just *knew*. She could have told Officer McDaid about the little knitted owl on the woman's dashboard, or the way her fingernails were painted red, the same as her lipstick, like you would if you were going out on a date. And Bonnie could have told the police officer that the young man's shoelaces were untied, long and white and just inviting disaster.

"You wouldn't be trying to keep this story for the newspaper, would you?" He says this like it's a joke, but with something underneath it, an insult Bonnie might be too stupid to understand.

She's disappointed he'd even suggest a low-life thing like that and she's about to tell him so when the lion pinches her just below her ribs. "I believe in the law, Officer," she says instead, trying not to wince so he doesn't think she's lying.

The fuzzy residue in her throat is nearly choking her and Bonnie coughs to clear it. She drinks from her glass of milk, which is now too warm and makes her think about a bad case of diarrhea she once had. She stands but Officer McDaid waves her back down. "Did you want some milk? Coffee? Tea? I didn't even ask." Bonnie feels breathless, disoriented. Officer McDaid seems younger than she originally thought, and not as pleasant-looking. "I don't know what's happening to me. Rudeness is inexcusable. Politeness. Decency. That's the hallmark of society. Without those, everything just falls to pieces. That's what my mother used to say."

Bonnie drinks the rest of the milk in one gulp.

"So the sound of their voices woke you up?"

Bonnie nods. The lion scratches at the back of her eyeballs and, inexplicably, simultaneously dances on her stomach. She closes her eyes. "That's all I know," she says. She keeps her eyelids glued together until she hears the door of her apartment shut behind Officer McDaid.

Bonnie pours a half-inch of pink antacid into a juice glass, gets into bed, and sips at it while she thumbs through the channels on TV. "You'd think they'd get a reporter out here lickety-split." She taps on her stomach as if knocking on a friend's door, like you see people do on TV, always running back and forth across the hall or a well-clipped lawn, sometimes not even bothering to knock before they barge in on their neighbors. "People are a constant disappointment," she says. She reaches behind and fixes her pillow, wiggles her toes under her sky-blue sheets. She thinks the lion has fallen asleep but then he squeezes her liver and she feels hot pain like a car door closing on her pinky finger. Tears sting her eyes. "Don't be mad at me."

Bonnie saw the woman with the fluffy blonde hair, her stick-thin arm out the window. She saw the young man in his electric blue running shorts, his hands on his hips, his body bent forward so they could talk. The way he smiled was like a wink with his mouth. He was beside the car and she was in it and at first they were just talking and Bonnie thought maybe the woman had stopped to ask for directions. But then the young man paced away from the car, and the woman yelled something, and he made a face and yelled back. There were words like *lover* and *love* and *married* and Bonnie leaned over and switched off her fan. She felt a thumping on her chest so she slid her hand down the front of her mint-green nightie and pressed her fingers to the skin over her heart.

They went back and forth like that, yelling at each other in a way that reminded Bonnie of her parents. She shook the thought out of her head and told herself that bad thoughts lead to bad deeds. She was relieved to see the young man walking away in a long circle that brought him to the front of the car. Bonnie tried to make it clear to Officer McDaid that she wasn't the kind of woman who thought the worst of people so there was no way she could have imagined the woman would drive right into him. Yes, Bonnie saw the car accelerate and yes, she just sat there on her bed, looking out her window. She was waiting for the car to veer off sharply to the right or left, to drive away with maybe a honk of the horn or an obscene gesture out the window.

It was not until she saw the car slam into the backs of his legs that Bonnie finally understood what was happening, and by then it was too late. By then the young man had buckled forward and landed on the tar and the woman had her big head of wild hair thrown back against the seat of her car. From her window, Bonnie could see the young man's milky legs and the soles of his white running shoes, the laces streamed out on either side.

The lion is clutching at her ribcage now. Bonnie rolls onto her side, hoping to dislodge him, but his claws grip tighter and tighter until she can barely breathe. "What else was I supposed to do?"

Possibly she could have stopped it, if she banged on her window or shouted down that good people were trying to sleep. But she hadn't wanted to make herself obvious. And besides, she couldn't have known it was going to end up like the way it did. When she was growing up and her parents argued there would be just a few words, and a look, and then they'd go off down the hall and close their bedroom door and that would be that. They didn't stand in the street and expect other people to get involved in their business.

Without switching on her lamp, Bonnie feels her way along the flocked wallpaper to the bathroom. In the bluish light of her nightlight she pulls her nightie into a handful just below her chest and with her free hand tugs her underpants down below her belly button. She looks at the baggy flesh of her stomach, the line of dark hair. She expected something more, the skin pulled tight like it would be for a baby. The lion is new but he isn't small and she thought she'd be able to see the outline of a paw, or maybe his rump pressed outwardly against her flesh. She lowers her nightie, opens her mouth wide and leans in closer to the mirror. No yellow fur or long teeth—nothing but her own silver fillings and the stain from the blueberry pie she had at dinner.

Bonnie calls in sick to work three days in a row. On the fourth, her boss tells her they've got a temp willing to fill in for her, if she'll be much longer. She wears her loose purple Aztec-print skirt and white peasant blouse because it's the only thing she owns that feels roomy enough for her and the lion. The minute she enters the newsroom, she sees a potted plant on the edge of her desk and the lion swishes his tail through her heart. But then she sees it's not a gift of welcome back, it's just her cactus, moved to the wrong side, as if someone has been sitting at her desk, going through her things.

Bonnie sits with her cup of tea and her list of people to call. Her pens are lined up, red to black to blue, and her notepad is unlined and ready. She expected everyone would be so eager to know about the accident they'd meet her at the door, offer to get her tea, pull out her chair for her. She imagined them sitting on the edge of her desk, legs crossed comfortably, diligently taking notes. They'll probably want to run a feature on her, with a picture. She takes out her compact and smoothes her eyebrows down with a wetted thumb.

People are getting coffee, or sending faxes, or heading off to their cars to go call on customers. Bonnie looks up from her desk, trying to keep her expression pleasant, neutral, un-expectant. The girl with the black hair and nose ring waves. The guy with the plaid shirt stops by and asks her if she had a nice vacation. "It wasn't exactly a vacation," Bonnie says, but he's already past her, punching buttons on the fax machine. Bonnie's boss stays in her office with the door closed. At noon, Bonnie knocks on the door. "I'm going to get lunch," she says. Her boss shoos her without looking up. Bonnie walks to CVS and buys a bag of pretzels and Skittles. She sits back down at her desk, shoves her purse into her desk drawer, and, after a few deep breathes to center herself, picks up the phone to call Turtle Trees about their ad. The lion paces through her gallbladder, her heart, her lungs. She puts down the phone and lays her head on her desk.

No one says anything when she leaves. On her way home, the lion presses on her bladder, her stomach, her throat. He sits on her chest, claws at her tongue, pokes her in the ribs, the liver, the spot at the back of her knees. The lion twists her muscles into knots and bites at them. She is trembling as though she's been remade of jelly and she can barely catch a single breath. In the bathroom, she fumbles through the medicine drawer for aspirin, shakes two into her palm, and washes them down with a swig from the tap. She waits, head tipped back, feeling the pills slide down her throat. She imagines them sinking into the lion like bullets, right into his chest, little explosions. But then she feels the ping of an aspirin against the lining of her stomach, and the pong of the other being lobbed back up her throat.

The way in would likely be the way out, and Bonnie puts a hand to her throat, considering. Shrinking him first seems the best way to go. Bonnie tries more aspirin and other over-the-counter pills as well as several leftover pain pills from when she had her appendix out. She also tries a variety of the home-spun remedies her mother used to use when Bonnie had an upset stomach: a cup of ginger tea, a spoonful of caraway seeds, mint gum. When none of that works, she balances herself on her head on a pile of pillows with her legs propped against her bedroom wall. The tea, gum, and seeds race up her throat and Bonnie gags, flings herself onto her side, and lies there on her bedroom floor, exhausted. The lion shakes his head and Bonnie feels food and drink stick in spots all over her insides.

She thinks of the zoo after she has drunk one-third of the bottle of purple-red cough syrup.

Her father used to take her to the zoo on Sundays, when divorced fathers took their kids, even though her parents were still married. They'd walk arm and arm past the lynx, the snow leopard, the black bear, the yak. In the bird exhibit, her father would whistle to the birds then cup a hand over his ear.

"They're talking back, Bonnie-blue. What are they saying?"

"That the monkeys want us," Bonnie responded, always, and her father would grab her around the waist and they'd run, linked together, until they arrived in front of the monkeys, laughing. Her father would clap, and twirl around, and scratch under his arms and when a monkey mirrored his movements, Bonnie's father would bow down low, one hand clasped at his waist, and thank the monkeys for coming. After her father left, Bonnie saved her allowance and bought giant bags of peanuts in their shells. She hid them under her bed and every night she crushed the shells in her hands, held them to her nose, and breathed deeply.

It's the kind of day with a damp gray fog that hovers over everything and so the zoo is practically empty. At the lion exhibit, Bonnie presses herself up against the glass and peers into the landscape of yellow dirt, thin bushes, and big rocks. "It's a nice place," she whispers, tipping her head downward toward her stomach where she can feel the lion stretched out among the cough syrup.

She pats her stomach through her loose, silky skirt. "Wake up, sleepy head." She cups her stomach in her hands and shakes it like a snow globe. She feels the lion stir. "Home sweet home," she says.

The lion digs his claws into the lining of her stomach. Bonnie presses her forehead against the sticky glass.

Bonnie's parents argued at a near crescendo, at times. Especially on the weekends when neither of them had to get up for work the next morning. Sometimes Bonnie could hear the slap-thud of things being thrown against the bedroom walls and she would force herself to listen and try to identify the objects. A book was easy, especially if it was something hardbound or heavy like the bible her father kept in his bedside drawer. Other things were harder to figure out—a watch, a wooden hanger. A porcelain figurine Bonnie had given her mother, but which one? The skinny giraffe painted yellow with perfectly round black spots? Or the clear elephant with the single blue jewel in the center of his forehead? Sometimes her parents did not emerge from their bedroom after a fight and Bonnie would sit on her bed all night, her bedroom door wide open and waiting, and she would imagine them bleeding to death on their nice gray carpets.

Unaware of the gathering zoo crowd, Bonnie sticks her head down her shirt. "I know you don't want to leave me," she says. "But you really have to."

She untucks her head from her shirt, lifts her arms above her head, and jumps, just like she and her father used to do in front of the monkeys. She feels the lion's claws loosen. She jumps again and again, her shirt billowing up and out. She can feel the lion, loose and unsettled inside her. She can hear her father, laughing but not disappointed.

She shakes her hips like her parents used to do, when they were getting along and they'd dance in the living room with the record player playing Fats Domino and Chubby Checker. Bonnie twists and bounces and the lion climbs into her head. She shakes her head, side to side and back and forth and up and down. Her hair is wild and streaming into her mouth and when she opens her eyes everything is red. The lion slides toward her ear and a second later Bonnie feels the tail slide out like a piece of cotton. A hind leg is next, full and heavy and pulling her ear apart. She squeezes her eyes shut and thinks about what her mother used to say about pain lasting only a few seconds before numbness sets in. Bonnie shakes her head faster and finally out falls his rump, his torso, and his great, hulking head.

Bonnie opens her eyes in time to see a great streak of light across the peanut-shelled tar.

It is not Officer McDaid who comes to get her but another police officer with gray-green eyes and the faint smell of popcorn on his clothes. He says, "Some people said they heard you growl."

Rubbery-tired, Bonnie leans into his shoulder and lets him lead her to his cruiser. "I don't think that was me," she says. The officer puts his hand over her forehead and helps her bend into the backseat and she thinks there are just no words for how kind people can be, when they're trying.

"People get upset when they have little kids around and someone's lifting up her shirt, dancing all over creation, making noises. You understand?"

Bonnie nods. "No one wants a loose lion." She stretches out on the warm backseat and closes her eyes. She feels wonderfully empty. Eventually, she lets the hum of the car's engine lull her to sleep.

Potomac

Andrew Payton
Iowa State University, MFA

When people ask about his face, Chepe likes to blame Reagan and the '89 invasion. A brick, he says, flew from the wall and through his pretty face. But in truth Chepe was seven when Noriega fell, and a year later when our family moved to the US and I was born stateside, it was still twelve years before he got the bullet, when I was thirteen and he was twenty-one and had lived most of his life on American soil. When the bagger at the grocery asks, and he does his bit about the bricks and bombs, she reaches out like she's going to fill the hole with her hands all pink and white, asking, "Does it hurt?" And for a second I think he's going to let her—she's got kind of a crooked face, too—but then her blue-vested manager steps in, says "Kristy," all stern and low, and she goes back to putting our eggs and milk in plastic bags.

It's a couple of blocks to the house where Chepe and I live together in Langley Park, where I've been since Ma kicked me out of her place once I dropped my classes at Maryland, and we're walking now, both because gas is up and since Chepe says I need the exercise. But sometimes I think it's worse breathing in this neighborhood. All smoke and pavement, insects and humidity—it's terrible, this place in summer. I'm rotting through my t-shirt and Chepe's got two beads of sweat hanging off the cliff of his spotty eyebrow, contemplating the jump into that purple void where his cheek and eye used to be.

When we get back we unload the groceries and he starts getting out bowls and measuring cups for the cake. I stand for a minute looking at him, then ask if he needs any help.

"Yeah, Ramon, we forgot the beer," he says.

So I go back out into the street headed the other way to cross the lot of weeds and gas station parking lots to the liquor store, even though I've already soaked my whole shirt, even though he never said anything before about wanting the beer. Making birthday cake was Chepe's idea. He didn't say why he wanted to bake something for the first time in I-don't-know-how-long, but I could take a pretty good guess: A few days from now it will be one year since he let our nephew José drown in the Potomac River on his birthday.

At some point the kid had seen people in kayaks under the bridges downtown, and for months Chepe promised that for his birthday they'd get out boats from this rental place in Georgetown. We all went: Maria, our older sister and José's mother, Chepe, me, and even Ma, who never leaves the house much anymore. Only Maria didn't feel like boats because she'd just been dumped by Victor the Mexican, and I don't know how to swim, and even though Chepe tried to get me in the water, saying, "You don't need to swim to sit in a piece of plastic and paddle, gordo," I stood on the dock with Maria and Ma and we waved as they floated off.

José was nine that day, smiling, and about an hour later Chepe came running down the road, wet and out of breath, made the boat people call 911, and just told us, "He flipped. River's too strong." Maria said nothing, just started running downriver, Ma and I huffing to keep up.

They found José's body two days later washed up in Northern Virginia, all swollen and blue. About every Latino in all of DC and Maryland came down to the river to hold a vigil, saying prayers and leaving candles to burn wax on the rocks. It was even on the news. Everybody except Chepe—he stayed at home, said he couldn't go see that river. That night I went over to his place just to sit with him and not say nothing. There was some reality show on TV where people were diving into a fake shipwreck after some fake chest of gold. When Maria barged in and found us like that, she started yelling. "My baby," she said. "You blind, motherfucker."

Two weeks later when classes started up again, I couldn't go. I was the only one who was going to see Chepe, the only one who cared enough to make him go to work, to make him eat or do anything besides drink and sleep. And so I dropped out, got kicked out of Ma's house, and took a job at the thrift store with Chepe, loading old couches onto people's cars and sorting through boxes of moth-eaten sweaters.

By the time I'm back, Chepe has already got egg whipped and butter melted and is measuring sugar and flour. I set the twelve-pack on the counter and we both crack one open. He doesn't want my help with the cake, so I just stand there drinking beer.

A few months ago our grandpa in Panama died and left the cattle ranch he'd worked his whole life to our childless uncle, and so Maria decided she would move back and learn cows. "I need change, Ramon," she told me. "I can't give to this place no more." She called Chepe a few weeks ago and said she wanted to talk. Since then he's been meaner than usual, getting on me about my weight and not telling me where he goes when he leaves.

Once Chepe gets the cake in the oven, we sit down in front of the television with half of the twelve pack already gone. Chepe takes his pocketknife off his hip and digs its point into the coffee table as I flip the channels.

"Where are you and Maria going?" I ask.

"Why, do you need to come along?" Chepe says, flicking a piece of laminate onto the floor. The table is scarred all over from this habit he has. He does it whenever he doesn't like what we're watching or is about to get angry with me for something. "Fucking mess," he says, and knocks an empty Big Gulp from the table to the floor. "I can't believe you drink that shit."

I find an old Batman movie, and as we watch, Chepe starts muttering to himself in Spanish, quicker than I can follow. When the oven timer rings, he gets up, finisher his beer, and throws it across the room for the trash. He misses and a bit of beer leaks onto the floor. He wraps his hands in a dish towel and moves the cake on the counter, and I follow the smell into the kitchen. "Looks good, man," I say. "It got all fluffy."

"Don't be so hungry, gordo," he says. "We got to ice it first."

Chepe goes into the grocery bags and gets out the tub of white icing, breaks the plastic seal, dips in a butter knife and lays a hunk onto the cake. Only the cake is too warm and as he moves the knife across, it rips the flesh up with it. Chepe keeps trying and when the hard icing has pockmarked the cake, he throws his fist down on the counter, says, "Fuck me."

"Want me to try?" I ask.

He drops the knife and goes into his bedroom. I start icing the cake, going at it a little slower and it works alright. Whenever Chepe gets mad like this I try to remember how he used to be, and that usually he'll switch off and apologize before too long. I know there's no science to it, but sometimes I think some people are born with debts to pay. Maybe because of who their parents were or some bad history they carry, but for some people it never lets up. They keep paying every day and somehow only get deeper in the hole.

That's what I think about Chepe sometimes. After he got shot, I sort of felt like the world owed him a fatass paycheck for taking a bullet meant for someone else. All those years too, growing up and staying out of the mess knocking on every door in the neighborhood, and Chepe's the one who's got to pay. When I was a kid he was the one who told me who I couldn't hang out with, and after our father left, he was the one who'd smack me across the mouth for saying shit to Ma or Maria. "You don't know what this family gives for you, Ramon. How much you have. Be grateful, hermano. You got to be grateful."

Ma and I heard the gunshot that night. We were watching TV, and Chepe was supposed to be home from his job at the McDonald's, when an ambulance passed our house and stopped on the corner. Ma wanted me to stay inside because I had school the next day, but I didn't listen and went out to where the paramedics were stringing up police tape around some dude face down in his own blood.

I kept looking around in the crowd for Chepe, until I recognized him from his uniform. When the paramedics loaded him onto the stretcher I could see his face had been opened wide, the bullet parting everything from his eye to his ear. On the pavement a pool of blood streamed towards the sewer drain. You could even hear the drip, what was a few minutes ago part of his body joining the leaves and trash down there. On the curb some Boy Scouts had spray painted in blue stencil, *DRAINS TO CHESAPEAKE BAY.* Since I knew it was Chepe, and I couldn't look at the ambulance anymore, I just stood there watching his blood go down that drain. I thought about where it was going, imagined its whole journey to the ocean—from Chepe's bloodstream to the sewer, creek to the river, bay to the ocean—and then the ambulance closed its doors and took his body away.

Chepe was in a coma for two weeks and then another two of just twisting in the sheets before he could come home from the hospital, and even then he couldn't work or get out of bed much and had to go back and forth to the doctors as they began to reconstruct his face. Ma paid every bit she had and all she could take out, and Maria too and her money she'd saved for college, and still it wasn't enough. When Chepe woke up I asked him who did it, but he couldn't remember anything about that night, and didn't know anybody who'd want to shoot him either. Just the same random stupid shit that always happens here. For a while I was asking people at school and in the neighborhood. Just be glad he ain't dead, they all said.

Though the bandages didn't cover his good eye he would get headaches so bad he couldn't really watch TV or anything, so for a few weeks every day after school I would read to him in bed. Together we made lists and I would go to the library and bring home giant stacks of books. We read the ones I wanted, like *Lord of the Rings* and *Dune*, but Chepe got bored with that and wanted to know stuff about history—"Read me something real," he said—about what was in this place before we were here, what the land looked like before the city, and so I got out these books about the Indians and the first white people.

We learned, and became obsessed with for a while, that there was this big Indian Chief named Powhatan who was so badass that all the villages that used to be from the Potomac to the middle of Virginia had to come to the river with corn or tobacco, deer hide or beads, and offer it up to Powhatan as tribute. And that's what the name Potomac means: The Place to Which Tribute is Brought. When the first white people landed, John Smith and his handful from England, Powhatan showed up with a string of scalps and said that if they wanted to live in his territory, they'd have to pay tribute, too. And so they did—for a while at least. The white people gave hatchets, bells, beads, and copper just so Powhatan didn't come with fire and arrows and send them back to England.

Chepe loved this. He loved to think of the Indian owning on white dudes. For a few months everything we thought badass we called 'Powhatan.' Though Chepe would get bad headaches and sometimes curse everybody out just for asking him how he was, those days in there, when I'd just bring a chair into his room and read whatever books we had out from the library, were some of the best days I can remember.

"*Tú eres tan inteligentes, hermano,*" Chepe would say. "I'm so proud of you, Ramon."

Chepe never spoke Spanish with me much. Nobody did, even when I was little, because they thought I'd be smarter if I only spoke English. But I could pretty much understand, and I knew he said it in Spanish because he meant it.

When Chepe comes out of his room, I've got the cake iced, even written 'Happy Birthday José' on it in icing from a blue squeeze tube. "You've got shitty handwriting," says Chepe, and he punches me in the chest, which is what he does when he's sorry. He doesn't say anything about the cake being written out to José; I guess he never thought I'd think otherwise.

"Least I can spell," I say.

"Touché," he says, "You right about that. I am one dumb motherfucker."

We're out of beer now and so Chepe checks the time on the microwave and asks if I want to go get a bottle. I take a scoop of the leftover icing into my mouth and grab my wallet from the end table by the couch, which has been my bed these days.

The bugs outside are screaming and I can smell a grill in somebody's back-yard. We pass an apartment complex where we hear a couple fighting through an open window. Satellites blink overhead. On a porch ahead a few kids sit on overturned milk crates, an older one throwing rocks at the brick wall of the house. As we're passing the kid with the rocks sees us and laughs, pointing us out to the others. Chepe stops and turns his body towards them. "What?" he asks.

"Keep moving, ugly bitch," says one of the kids, who can't be more than twelve.

"Say that again, you little black fucker," says Chepe. He puts his hand on his hip where I know he's got his knife.

"Hey, come on, Chepe, let's go," I say.

"Best listen to your fat bitch," the kid with the rocks says.

"Chepe." I'm trying not to look at these kids. This is the kind of shit I did when I was their age. Nothing given to you, just pushing until you find what's yours to take. "Let's go, man." Chepe says something in Spanish about Panama and spits into the grass, but he turns and follows me, and the kids start laughing as we walk away.

At the liquor store we buy a bottle of vodka from the guy with the turban, who doesn't look us in the eyes as he counts our change, just shouts something to a guy in the back with thirty-packs on a handcart. I screw the top off the bottle as soon as we leave the store and hand it to Chepe, who takes a drink and hands it back.

I've got another two years left at Maryland, and lately Maria's been on me to finish. Ma never did more than kick me out, but Maria told me they're always talking about it: "We can lead your ass to water, but we can't make you drink." I was taking classes in business and history, my grades always just enough to pass. I don't know if I will start up again, it just doesn't seem worth the loans I'd need to take out, especially if Maria leaves for Panama and isn't here to push. I thought for a little while about going back with her, even if I don't know a thing about cows; it seemed like something other than this, other than Langley Park and Chepe, but then I just thought *back?* My whole family might be from Panama, but I grew up in three different apartments and two houses in a couple different neighborhoods, not speaking Spanish or English as good as anybody else, in this big stretch of pavement called the East Coast. *Back.* There is no back.

We get real drunk on vodka. Drunker than I think either of us have been in a long time, and before long Chepe's puking up in the bathroom. When he comes out he picks up his phone from the table and stares into the screen, his eye squinted and quivering.

"You got to make a phone call?" I ask.

"Yeah," he says. He leaves me and walks out the back door, leaving it wide open. After a few minutes I hear him talking real low and can see that he's sitting in the middle of the uncut grass. The streetlamps and porch lights mix with moon and cover him in different colors of light.

"You okay, hermano?" I ask him.

"I'm fantastic, gordo," he says. "I'm fucking fantastic."

Out on the main road a car burns its tire on a turn. He throws his phone into the air and catches it right before it comes down onto his face, and then he throws it up again but this time its arcs off into the bushes. Chepe doesn't get up to get it, just leaves it there. Inside the movie we were watching ends and an infomercial blares and shouts. I let him lie, and going inside, turn off the kitchen light and television, leaving him alone in the dark.

The doorbell rings and I wake with a headache, everything a bit off key. I pull on some shorts and go to answer the door. It's Maria: she's done up way too nice for whatever time it is, and when she hugs me and I smell her fruity shampoo and perfume, I realize how I must smell to her. She comes in, twisting car keys in her hands and staring around at the fast food trash and the stain on the ceiling where the roof leaks. "Is Chepe here?"

"Yeah, I'll go get him."

I knock on Chepe's door, "Maria's here, man." I hear a groan on the other side and so I go in and shut the door behind me. Chepe's room smells bad like always and I walk over a layer of clothes and trash to get to his bed. The plastic curtain is pulled down and the only light in the room is the square of sun that comes in around the edge. "Get up, dude, it's Maria."

"Fuck, Ramon, I'm sick."

"Yeah, I know, me too, but Maria's here."

He sits up in bed and I tug on the curtain so that it rolls up into itself to show the bright green square of backyard. "Why do you have the window closed? It's hot in here."

"Those bugs are too loud."

I push up on the window for a bit a fresh hot air. I throw Chepe a pair of pants from the floor and he drops his legs into them. I find a shirt, too, one hung from the back of a chair that still looks fresh and he pulls that on.

We go into the hall and see that Maria is standing in the kitchen looking at the cake.

"Maria," Chepe says, his voice cracked and nasal.

"You made him a fucking cake?"

"Next week—"

"You don't think I know?"

Chepe doesn't say anything. I stay in the dark of the hall leaning against the wallpaper.

"You think it's still his birthday? He can eat this cake?" She shakes her head, flipping through the keys on her keychain. She speaks to him in Spanish about his face and the trash in the room. He just keeps saying "Si" in a broken voice until she stops.

"I'm sorry," she says in English, throwing her hands up in the air. "I can't do this."

"We didn't mean anything—" I start to talk, but Maria looks at me with all her anger shooting from her eyes before turning back to Chepe.

"I swear, you two don't do nothing but eat, shit, drink, and sleep. You sure are a good example for your brother, Chepe. You sure show him how to be a man. Just like Papa, both of you."

"Maria," Chepe says. She looks at him with her head cocked, impatient and trained on whatever he is about to say. He stays quiet for a moment. "Just—Maria."

"I wanted to tell you, Mama's coming back to Panama with me." I didn't know this. Ma never said anything about going back to Panama—but then I try and remember when's the last time I've gone over to see her. Weeks? Months?

"Panama?" Chepe asks, like he's never heard of the place.

"This place is no good. We're no good here."

She stares at us for another minute, then shakes her head and curses us in Spanish, leaving us standing there in our dirty clothes and hangovers, all the trash around our feet.

"Did you know Mama was going back?" Chepe asks me.

"She didn't tell me that."

"What are we supposed to do?"

"We'll get cleaned up, man," I tell Chepe. "She's not really mad about the cake. We'll say sorry."

"The fuck do you know, Ramon? What do you know about people?" Chepe kicks the trash at his feet as he walks towards the front door. He slams the door, but the lock doesn't catch and it swings open on the creaky hinge.

The night Chepe got shot, Maria drove us all to the hospital, Ma up front shouting at cars to get out of the way, and José in the back with me, strapped in his car seat. Chepe wasn't dead but in critical condition, all the machines and tubes running in and out of his body and nurses fluttering around. Maria was bouncing José in her arms. She was about twenty-four then, and José was a baby still and hadn't begun to put on all that weight that he'd eventually get when he was older. Ma was sat by Chepe's side, mumbling prayers, and Maria was rocking on her heals, saying, "Dios, Dios, Dios."

When Ma took a break from praying, Maria spoke to her, "You still think America is a safe place to raise a family?" Ma didn't say nothing, just bowed her head and picked up another prayer, every now and then kissing Chepe's limp hand. I remember wanting to call my father, thinking that someone should let him know. At that point it had been over a year since we'd seen him, but I don't know if anyone had a number anyway. No one even mentioned his name.

Maria set José in a chair and the boy laid his head on the armrest and grunted. She placed her hand on one of the machines invented to keep bodies alive and told me the only story I'd ever heard about the invasion. The whole time she spoke, Ma just nodded her head, not adding a word, but looking at me to confirm it was all true. "I was eleven when the bombs fell on Panama City," Maria said. "Papa took Chepe to the roof to watch the fires, and Mama took me into the basement. We could hear the explosions and see the dust fall from the floorboards above us. There were soldiers in the streets. Our father had wanted this all to come. He said it would be a good thing for Panama, that without Noriega we could have democracy."

I stood by the window watching her. She traced her fingers over the machines, along the wires to where they met their electricity. "A few minutes after they went to the roof, Chepe came down alone. He passed Mama by and came to me, putting his head in my lap. He didn't cry, but he stayed like that all night, and I did, too. 'Baby Chepe,' I said. 'Baby Chepe.'" Now she was stroking the bandage covering his head, Ma and her both crying and holding hands now, and under her breath Ma whispered another prayer in Spanish. I stayed by the window. They didn't ask me to join them, and I didn't know the prayers they both seemed to know, word for word. For what seemed like the whole night I looked out the window, watching the ambulance come to feed new bodies to the automatic doors.

Hours later Chepe's still gone. I go to work to cover a short shift at the thrift store, but I'm back in the evening and Chepe's still not home. The cake is on the counter, the icing getting hard, and so I decide that since I paid for the ingredients I am going to eat a slice. I've only had a bite, not even chewed, when Chepe walks in and sees me with the cake. He storms over to me and knocks the paper plate out of my hand. The fork flies away and rattles in the sink and the cake strikes me right in the chest, the icing sticking and the rest falling down my shirt to the floor.

What's your problem, man?" I start brushing it off and smear my hands in chocolate.

"Why didn't you tell me, Ramon?" Chepe says, pounding his fists on the counter and then bending his forehead between them.

"Tell you what?"

"The cake, man. How stupid are we, Ramon?"

"I don't know."

He looks up at me and sees the cake on my chest. "I'm sorry, brother. Fuck, I'm sorry."

I don't say anything back. I don't say it's okay. I want out right now. I can't be alone in America with Chepe, the rest of my family gone, disappeared. Outside the sun is going down. Chepe keeps his head down on the counter a long time, and I just stand there looking at him, not touching the cake on my shirt or on the floor. He's got a bald spot growing on the back of his head. I see now how skinny he is, not just not fat like me, but really skinny in an almost bad way. There are so many other people we could be at any given time—not Chepe and not Ramon, but some other two brothers someplace else away from all this. After a while Chepe lifts his head off the table, and his eye looks tired and dry.

"I need you to drive me to that river, Ramon. I need to see the river."

We drive through pools of streetlight, following the bends in Canal Road. A lightning bug flies into the windshield, its butt still lit up, and when we park the car in the dark of the lot, Chepe flicks it onto the pavement. We walk a concrete footbridge over the canal that the white people built to haul coal out of the mountains. The water is still now, nothing moves. The boathouse is closed, all boats in their sheds and locked away. We follow the gravel path where employees drag kayaks and canoes down to the water, and then turning away where it leads to the docks, we go straight through the grass to the shore of the river.

Chepe picks a spot and sits down so that the water is so close we could reach down and grab it. The air is full of bugs, and I realize that the birds filling the dark space over the river aren't birds at all, they're bats. I tell Chepe this.

"You remember Powhatan, Ramon?"

"The Chief of the River."

"The Motherfucking Boss."

Chepe reaches down and takes up a handful of wet dirt, and standing up, pitches it towards the river. "Here you go, Powhatan," he shouts. He does it again.

I work my fingers under a big stone and lift it out of the mud. I have to stand and heave my body to throw it out—it makes a hollow splash. The water rushes by. Headlights on the Virginia side occasionally break through the trees. We start picking up everything we can find—handfuls of gravel and dead logs, dry grass we pull out of the dirt—and we throw it all into the river.

"Hey, Powhatan," Chepe taunts.

I shout with Chepe. We're both shouting.

"You hear me, you motherfucker?" Chepe throws a handful of gravel and I can hear that he's breathing hard. "What else you need, huh?"

He falls back into the grass and mud and I sit beside him. In the light of the boathouse I can see Chepe's face—the bad side—and he's smiling.

"You know this eye can still see, Ramon?"

"Yeah?"

"It looks at things the other one can't." Everything we threw in the river has sank or floated away. The purple flesh circles around his dull eye like a tornado, like bathwater in a tub. I try and see what Chepe sees. There's a whole village of people here holding nothing, gathering up for the long walk home, and I imagine the chief and his train of armed guards, their canoes loaded with bounty, paddling south in the dark.

"Potomac" was a finalist for the Nelson Algren Award
and was published in *The Chicago Tribune*.

Coffee for Dead Children

Zoe Vandeveer
UC Irvine, MFA

Amy has never been to a wake before, and she doesn't know what to say or bring or wear or do. She doesn't want to go. She would rather spend the afternoon on the couch, cutting her cuticles and catching up on Law and Order. She worries their presence will be awkward, that people will think they're rubberneckers, that their very aliveness will be an affront to death. Mainly she's afraid that all that sadness will find some undefended crack in her exterior and work its way inside.

"Can't we just send flowers?" she asks Greg. He's in the walk-in closet picking out something to wear, and she watches him from the bed. It's nearly one and she's still in her robe. Since they moved out here whole days will pass without her getting properly dressed.

"No, Amy," he says. "We're going. It's the neighborly thing to do." He has so many shirts and all he ever wears are scrubs. He flips quickly through his clothes, his fingers briefly alighting on each sleeve. She wonders why he can't use his eyes to process information like a normal person. Why must he always touch everything? They've been married almost two years, and the tics she thought she'd get used to still baffle her. She repositions her robe so that one nipple pokes out, and gives it a pinch to make it erect. It's a cheap trick, but she'll try anything to delay them.

"Do you think he'll recognize me in civilian clothes?" Greg asks, still examining the shirts. He's a medical equipment salesman and his new territory includes the father's hospital. On the bed, she splays open her legs, but he still hasn't looked over at her.

"Maybe I should wear a light blue Oxford."

"We've got to dress up for this thing?" she says. He puts on the blue shirt and inches a tie tight around his neck. She drops the robe and walks naked to the closet, a final attempt at derailment. He slaps her on the butt on his way out the door and down the stairs, his footsteps muffled by the cream carpeting that covers their world like an expensive moss. She rests her head against the closet door for a moment before putting on her frumpiest outfit, a gray shift dress she bought in the hopes of interviews for creative, well-paying jobs. When she enters the kitchen, Greg is frowning at the coffee maker which is threatening to overflow.

"Coffee? That's what we're bringing?" Amy asks. He gives her a look down the length of his nose. "Shouldn't we bring something the boys would have actually enjoyed?"

"The coffee is for me and the rest of the grown-ups, Amy."

"You don't have to be a dick about it. I'm making pie." Greg looks at the clock that hangs over the stove. "To honor their memories," she adds.

"Babe, we can't be late to this sort of thing." They stand on either side of the faux granite island and stare at each other. Amy gets out the mixing bowls and lines them up. She can't remember the last time she baked.

"We'll go when the pies are done. I'm making two, one for each of the boys." She looks at the cans she alphabetized last week and decides on pumpkin, even though it's April and the frozen earth is starting to soften. He watches as she whisks in the eggs and the milk, as she realizes her mistake — pumpkin pies are quick, you don't even have to par-bake the crust. As she's putting them in the oven Greg comes over and slides a hand up her skirt.

"How long do they have to bake?" he asks. She sets the timer for forty minutes and he carries her back up the stairs where they undress and fuck for a while until the pies are ready.

⸻

Greg thinks they should walk, the Roberstons live one cul-de-sac over, but Amy insists on driving. She doesn't want their cheeks to be rosy with good health when they arrive.

"You've really never been to a wake? What about a funeral?" Greg asks as the car moves too slowly down the street. The development has just put in a row of speed bumps and she can feel a layer of stomach fat jiggle with each forward lurch of the car. The pies are still hot in her lap. She shakes her head no, but he won't let it go. "Really? You've made it to the ripe old age of twenty-four and not a single person you know has died?"

Amy flips through her memory for likely candidates but all her grandparents are alive and everyone she knows is seemingly impervious to terminal illnesses and fatal accidents. Then a grey memory of her high school Italian teacher surfaces: a death after a short battle with some sort of cancer. The school held a memorial assembly for her a few days after she'd died. Amy walked into the gym and saw the rest of her class sitting in the front row of the bleachers, holding hands and looking brave, and she decided to spend the period in the girls' locker room practicing sad faces in the mirror and pinching herself until she cried. At dinner her mother had told her that Italian was a stupid language to learn anyway, and Amy transferred into beginning Spanish and put the whole thing behind her.

"Guess I'm just lucky," she says now to Greg, and it's this luckiness that worries her. She knows that no life can go untouched by misfortune, so she's stockpiling emotions for her own tragedy that has yet to reveal itself. She'll spend hours thinking about her mother dying in a plane crash; she'll picture the somber state troopers who will knock at her door after Greg is killed in a five-car pile up on his way to work. It's her way of training for trouble, but it means that she finds herself lacking in situations like this. She hasn't prepared for this scenario and doesn't trust herself to feel the right feelings.

A row of dark cars are parked outside the Robertson's, and Amy elbows Greg to say: see, everyone drove. Greg rings the doorbell and when the father answers it's much worse than she expected. He's shrunken in his grief and she senses there's a new, crueler clock on his body. She's never formally met Mr. Robertson, but she's seen him mowing his lawn on Saturdays. She's admired the rope of his arms and has spent not a few minutes thinking of his surgeon's fingers and how his muscles must flex when he's touching his wife or tucking his kids into bed. She can't reconcile that person with the being in front of her now—Mr. Robertson had been a real man, someone she imagined smelled of no-nonsense soap and bourbon. He could have been Paul Newman or Marlon Brando, but now his flesh seems ready to give up its grasp on his bones and this is sadder than anything. Amy looks down at her shoes, nude patent stilettos, entirely inappropriate for the occasion.

"We're so sorry for your loss," Greg is saying, and Amy and the father both know he means it. Greg has a more developed capacity for caring than she does. That's the main reason she married him: for his goodness and because she thought he could help pull her outside of herself and into a life of bigger things, other people. But she's starting to realize that the adult world is programmable coffee makers and obligations you keep out of a sense of decency and not because you want to.

"Those poor sweet boys," Amy says to the father and accidentally smiles. He looks at her for a moment before resuming his rhythmic nodding. She thinks she should reach across and pat his arm but she's got a pie in each hand. On the front step she sees the morning's paper still in its plastic wrapper, which means they haven't yet seen the article on the front page of the Local section. She read it over breakfast, tracing her finger over the black-and-white school portraits of the boys, their cowlicks and toothless smiles capturing a simulacra of the pure goodness of youth.

The tragedy is this: the boys were playing with their friends in their treehouse when the youngest, aged six, decided to climb even higher. He had just swung a leg onto the next branch when he slipped and sailed past his older brother, aged eight, and unnamed neighborhood children who were all playing a card game in the treehouse. The older brother reached for him and fell, striking his head on a new marble water feature. He died instantly. The youngest seemed fine at first, but he died later that night from a rupture in his brain. A bleed so small the doctors didn't find it until it was too late. Mr. Robertson had spent the month of June building the treehouse—Amy had monitored his progress with interest—and she wondered how much worse that makes it for him. Is there an upper limit on tragedy, or does it continue to build with each fresh horror?

"Thank you for coming," the father says like he is repeating an expression he doesn't understand. They nod at him a few more times, all of them bobbleheads now, and show themselves through the foyer and into the living room. They know the house—it's the Jefferson, the same model as theirs.

"I knew we shouldn't have come," Amy whispers in the relative hush of the corridor. "We're just making it worse."

The Robertsons have better taste than she would have thought, more urban and sophisticated than the rest of Valley Meadows, and Amy feels a new sorrow that comes with the near spark of missed friendship. These people could have been their people. Amy has spent the last four months coming to terms with being friendless and alone for the next three years. Three years of Greg selling endoscopy and arthroscopy equipment and they can move back to New York and buy a condo. Amy can get back into PR. Three years and they'll be off to a great start. That was how Greg had put it, like they were racehorses. Amy had agreed because she hated the realities of entry-level work, the endless spread-sheets and the pay stubs that always seemed like they should be bigger. Greg had said he had an opportunity to make real fuck-you money. But it's lonelier here than she had thought, more isolating. When the regional VP of Lyfker Medical offered Greg a good deal on a house in a half-developed development they had jumped at it. "You'll love it, just don't forget the milk," the VP had said. They'd laughed, and it was only after the movers had finished unloading their boxes in the double-high foyer did they understand—the nearest store is twenty-seven miles away.

They find Mrs. Robertson in the kitchen, surrounded by the other mothers who can empathize in a way that Amy cannot. Greg and Amy hand Mrs. Robertson the thermos of coffee and the two pies, and she too nods her head as she receives their offerings. Greg tells her it's special coffee, from a single estate grower in Guatemala, and she holds it tighter. Amy puts the pies on an island already laden with casseroles and pasta dishes. She tells Mrs. Robertson the pies are her grandmother's secret recipe. In truth it's just the recipe from the back of the can and she doesn't know why she lies.

"Pumpkin has powerful antioxidants," one of the other mothers says. She gives Amy a funny look, and they all stare at the food because no one knows what to say. The kitchen counter is very clean. In the silence Amy remembers that she once had a pet mouse, Sunny, who died unexpectedly when she was seven. Amy had left her Halloween candy under her bed so her mother wouldn't make her throw it away and the mouse had gotten into it and eaten too much. She and her best friend had put on black t-shirts and dark denim overalls and made sad faces as her mother dug a grave in the backyard and told them that everyone and everything dies sooner or later. Amy didn't cry until a week later when a raccoon dug up the tissue box coffin, shreds of cardboard scattered across the lawn.

Amy's next-door neighbor, Mrs. Hardin, grabs her by the elbow and steers her to the picture window in the dining nook. Amy's first thought is that she wishes she and Greg had such a large window, too, but then she sees what Mrs. Hardin is looking at: the treehouse proud in the oak tree, leaves just starting to bud and a few pieces of yellow police tape stuck to the bark. Amy and Greg have a couple of saplings languishing in their back yard, and she realizes that no one has mature trees. Valley Meadows was built in the High Plains, sad scrub brush stretching for knotty miles. The Robertson's tree must be the only old tree around, and Amy wonders what strong seed blew in on what wind.

"It's a nice tree," Amy says. "I hope they chop it down."

"Those were lovely boys," Mrs. Hardin says. "Such a tragedy. So devastating to the community."

"You knew them well?" Amy asks. She and Greg had never met the boys. They'd seen them racing on bikes or skateboards or rollerblades—they had endless wheeled means of careening around the cul-de-sac, and Greg would mutter that they were going to get run over one of these days. He'd say: haven't their parents ever taught them about sidewalks? She'd liked the way their exuberance couldn't be contained within safe boundaries. She'd watch their faces, boredom and glee trading places as rapidly as the weather systems that came down over the Rockies. She thought about joining them and the other kids sometimes, getting them to teach her how to skateboard or where to dig for arrowheads in the soft mounds of that marked old Indian encampments.

"I babysat for them once when the second boy was just a baby," Mrs. Hardin says with pride. She's here to partake in the communal suffering so she can remind herself she still lives. She's the sort of woman who moves her sprinkler if she sees its water falling on a neighbor's lawn for free.

"Was that your career?" Amy asks. "Childcare?"

"No dear, I was a housewife. Marty always had a good job, and when he passed he had good life insurance." She keeps staring at the tree. "I bought one of these brand new houses and decorated in pretty pinks and yellows top to bottom." Amy studies her nails because she can't bring herself to look at the casseroles or the tree or Mrs. Hardin. "Everyone in Valley Meadows is so lovely," Mrs. Hardin says. "Don't you think?"

"Excuse me," Amy says. She looks around for Greg, thinking he can rescue her, but he's no longer in the kitchen. None of the men are, and she sees this is part of the wake. The men go off to be men, the women to be women. She wonders whose approach is better.

Amy gets a glass of punch from a crystal bowl on the kitchen table and wishes it were spiked. One of the women nods at her from across the kitchen and Amy turns away. Greg has told her to not be so superior, but she feels so different from these women who dress in sweatshirts with sewn-in collars. They wear thin crosses on thinner gold chains that swing on the outside of blouses buttoned all the way up, and she tells Greg that is what putting on airs really looks like. She's tried to make friends. When they first moved to Valley Meadows she went to a meeting of the book club, but they never even opened the book. Now they watch her take her slow jogs around the development, her lungs drying out from the altitude. She is a different species, ill-suited for this environment.

A cry from somewhere in the house cuts through the kitchen, and Amy realizes she hasn't seen any of Valley Meadow's children here. All of the fathers and all of the mothers are present, but she's had no sense of living children. Everyone is quiet for a moment but the cry stops just as suddenly and the women return to their hushed huddles of three or four. If Amy had children she wouldn't have brought them to a wake, not this sort of wake, because it's too real and too sad. The boys' drawings are still tacked to the fridge. She wonders where the children are and what they are doing. Do they understand what has happened?

In the den she finds Greg. He's drinking a full glass of what looks like whiskey and everyone, even Mr. Robertson, is laughing at his story. Amy takes a seat in one of the folding chairs that was rented for the occasion. Greg's eyes catch on her but he keeps talking. It's a story she's never heard, something about the time he and his buddies decided to bring a donkey to his high school championship basketball game. The donkey went crazy at the cheerleaders' shiny pompoms, hee-hawing and bucking and shitting all over the place (and here Greg does an apt imitation, a few drops of whiskey sloshing over the side of his glass). She doesn't find it that funny, at least not as much as everyone else apparently does, but she can appreciate the relief Greg is offering them all. She wouldn't have thought such humor would be appropriate for the occasion, but Greg is working some sort of social magic that he must have learned in sales.

"Now, Dr. Roberston," he's saying, "I gotta tell the story about Mrs. Eckersley. Were you in the hospital a couple of weeks ago when all that went down?" Dr. Robertson nods yes, and it no longer looks like his head risks coming loose from his torso. Greg had told her this story over cheese soufflé last week, an older woman's terrifically funny reaction to anesthesia, so Amy tunes out the words and just watches Greg. When you live with someone, she thinks, you can't see the small ways they change every day. Greg is thicker and stronger through the middle than when they married. His face is lined with wrinkles around the eyes, and when he smiles a grin that splits his face wide and happy. He looks like a man, and she wonders if she's changed too. If he still sees a girl from Delta Gamma or if she's developed into something more.

They married the week after college graduation because Amy was pregnant. No one had time for condoms on Spring Break, all of them fucking like that week was all that was left in the world. She'd lost the baby a few days before she walked down the aisle, but to back out then would be to admit they were doing it because of the pregnancy. Her seamstress had been too busy to take in the extra fabric around her waist so she looked fat anyway, and at the reception she snuck vodka cranberries while her mother told her it was a blessing. Now she'd have a good husband and nothing to muck up the marriage. Amy had gotten upset and told her mother she was through with the unsolicited advice. If she needed any more hot tips she'd go to Greg—he was her family now. Her mother had slapped her lightly on each cheek.

"Haven't you learned to be tough yet?" she asked. "Haven't I taught you anything?" Her mother took two bottles of Cava and walked out of the ballroom, and Amy hitched her skirt so high her garter showed and danced like she was happy.

One of the other doctors starts on a new story, and she sees Greg slide his business card across the coffee table. That's another side of him she can't picture. Calm in the face of all that blood and fat slipping down suction tubes, thick staples punching through flesh, all the ugliness of the human body laid bare. But he's good at his job. He's already on track to meet quota. It makes her nervous, his success, that she married a man whose skill is to watch surgeries and explain how his various new stents work.

"Why aren't you in the kitchen?" Greg asks her quietly during a lull in the room. "With the other women?"

"Because it's not 1950. Because it's too goddamn sad in there. Because, speaking of God, they are all Jesus-loving drones who freak me out."

"I think you mean clones," Greg says and he's right. She takes the tumbler of whiskey from him and downs it in large, painful gulps. She hands him the empty glass and decides to go sit in the car and wait for him to finish whatever business he has at the Robertson's. But as she's crossing the foyer to the front door she hears something above her. A row of skinny legs dangle from the gaps in the banister. Next to them, a pudgy girl stands at the railing, her elbows pouting over the edge. She motions to Amy, who looks over her shoulder to make sure no one is watching. She has found the children, and they're giving off an air of the forbidden. Amy thinks it must be their way of coping with what has happened.

"Do you want to play with us?" the pudgy girl asks in a loud whisper. "It's so boring down there." The girl meets Amy at the bottom of the stairs and takes her by the hand. She is sticky. Amy knows that the second floor has three bedrooms, a master and two smaller rooms connected by an adjoining bathroom, so she is surprised when the pudgy girl leads her into the Roberston's room.

"Are we allowed in here?" she says, and feels foolish for asking permission from a child.

"We're only allowed in here," the girls says. Then, "I'm Beatrice and I'm in charge. I'm eight and a half on Sunday."

"I'm Amy. Pleased to meet you, Beatrice. And who are your friends?" Several children pop up from where they've been hiding behind the bed. They sit on the duvet, which is laid across the floor like a picnic blanket. One of the boys is trying to make a fort from the bed sheets—he's tied one corner to a bedpost and is trying to get another corner to stay taut between the window and the windowsill. Amy watches him as he slams the window over and over. The glass cracks. The boy looks at the fissure, which runs the length of the pane. He shrugs and the bed sheet falls slowly to the ground.

"I told you it wouldn't work, Peter P. You should have listened to me," Beatrice says. The younger children look back and forth between the two kids.

"Are we going to get in trouble?" asks one of the others. Amy thinks they range in age from three to six, but she's never been good at guessing how old children are.

"Course not," Beatrice says. "The Robertsons are too sad to care about dumb things like windows. Right, Amy?"

"Well, the good thing to do would be to tell them," Amy says. She feels the hot thread of a headache start to wind up her neck and around to her forehead.

"Sure. You go tell them, Amy. Say, sorry your kids are gone to heaven and we broke your window." Beatrice is staring at her, her hands crossed over her chest in challenge. Before Amy can say anything, Peter P. is pulling on her hand and pointing at the desk across the room. Beatrice says that he can't talk, but he wants her to move the desk over so they can finish their fort. Cold air has started to come in through the window.

"I'm just going to go find your parents," Amy says, but one of the smallest ones has closed the door and Amy feels fear tighten around her. She tells herself to stop being ridiculous, these are just children.

"Please play with us?" one of them says in a strangely high voice. "We're so bored. And sad." The whiskey is slipping into her blood and so she helps Peter move the desk closer to the bed. It's heavier than she expected. The sheets are some slippery material, and it takes her a few tries to secure the corner to the table leg to form a sagging sort of roof. One of the other kids brings in a high-backed chair that helps prop the sheet up a little, but it's a sorry fort. They all crawl in, the sheet resting on Amy's head. She can almost smell the static electricity gathering in her hair. It's dark under there, the air is hot and close.

"Are we going to start?" one of the little ones asks. Amy is trying to match them with the grown-ups downstairs, to suss out any siblings in the group, but they all seem so emphatically their own. Two of them take her hands, and she sees that they've arranged themselves in a circle and are all saying something Amy can't quite understand. She wants to laugh—she's found the only club in Valley Meadow's that seems to want her as a member.

"We've been watching you," Beatrice says. "Ever since you and your husband got here."

"Well, aren't you little sneaks." Amy is flattered, proud. They must see her as the cool, young woman from the city. They must recognize how she is different from their mothers. Amy remembers the ease of childhood imagination, how you could go all sorts of places so quickly. She's glad to be hanging out with these kids, away from the treacherous etiquette of the proceedings downstairs.

"In fact," Beatrice says solemnly. "We chose you as our leader. Do you accept?" Amy finally does laugh, but the sound echoes strangely under the sheet. Ever since that miscarriage she's thought there must be something fundamentally wrong with her. She's thought that she isn't cut out for children—they'd never gotten good at birth control and she'd never gotten pregnant again. Greg sometimes brings up trying for babies, especially since the Lyfker job, but she doesn't know if she's ready to be so tied down. These kids though, with their earnest faces, are making her want to reconsider. Right there in the fort she decides to make an appointment with a doctor at one of Greg's hospitals, get a workup to see what her options are. A preliminary thing. Amy moves a furtive hand to her stomach. They hadn't used protection this morning and maybe these children are a sign that she's finally ready for another baby.

"I'd be honored to," she says. "Do we have a club name?" One of the children starts crying, and then three of them are. Her eyes have almost adjusted to the light, and she's stunned by the quickness of their grief.

The littlest crawls into her lap and whispers, "We're the Bad Kids. That's the club."

"As our leader, you have to determine the punishment," Beatrice says.

"For the window?"

"For the dead children."

Amy can't quite figure out what Beatrice is talking about, and she moves the sheet aside to let in more light so she can see better. Seven faces are looking at her, waiting.

"Oh, Beatrice. That was a accident, what happened to those boys," she says slowly. "A terrible accident."

"No, Amy," Beatrice says, drawing out the vowels of Amy's name long and mean. "That's why we brought you here. Peter P. dared Will to climb to the top, and then Max pushed him off. His brother said he'd tell, so I pushed him off." Amy opens and closes her mouth a few times.

"What?" she says at last. The whiskey has made her mouth dry, and she licks her lips as she looks at the faces around her. The children are more upset than they'd seemed, she decides. They're working out their grief through this bizarre fantasy.

"An eye for an eye, right?" one of the little ones says. "That means Beatrice and Max have to die, too. And Peter P. has to do something scary, like climb real high."

"Yeah," says the one in her lap, squirming so that hard knees dig into her stomach. "You have to punish them and then they'll jump out of the treehouse. Or maybe the window, since we aren't allowed in trees anymore."

"Or the landing outside!" says another. Four of them are climbing on her now and she thinks this must be what drowning is like.

"Just tell us what to do, Amy. You're our leader. You're one of us."

"Okay," Amy says, the word pointy in her mouth. "Let's see now."

How To Like Girls

Courtney Gillette
Lesley University, MFA

Smile. Never judge a girl by the length of her hair. Don't believe the voice in your head that tells you all the good ones are taken. Go say hi. Tell her you like her tattoo. Ask her what she's been listening to. Hope that she says Sleater Kinney. Smile politely if she says Dave Matthews Band. Make sure your friends are watching so they can rescue you if it doesn't go as planned. Make sure she isn't actually interested in your friend. (It's happened.)

When you are seventeen, you will assault every attractive vaguely lesbian person by asking them their name and if they have a girlfriend. Relax. Learn to strike up a conversation. Then, casually mention your ex-girlfriend, which communicates that you are 1) gay and 2) single. Find out where she went to college. Laugh in such a way that you reach out and touch her arm, just slightly, just enough. Ignore what all the magazines you read as a teenager say about flirting. Never, ever bat your eyes, unless you want to convey that you've lost your contact lens. Don't lose your contact lens when you're flirting. It means you're trying too hard. In fact, stick with glasses. Trust your gut.

Sometimes, you won't even have to start the conversation, like when you are nineteen, and stare wistfully at a girl with a shaved head at your friend's art show, and later, at a bar in the East Village, the same shaved-head girl will materialize, approach you with a smirk, and say, *So you ditched the art gallery to hang out in a dyke bar, too?* Laugh. Agree to split a beer with her; you are nineteen and she is twenty-one and you are both broke. After you learn that she's an artist, lives in Brooklyn, saw a terrific cellist playing on the L train today, and is about to graduate from NYU, lean over the noise and heat of the bar and shout, *By the way, my name's Courtney.* Don't be surprised when she spits out her beer and says, *We have a problem. My name's Courtney, too.*

Laugh, the head back reckless kind of laugh, the kind that makes your mother think you're on drugs because who can cackle like that? Take the joint she passes you right there in the bar between your fingers and inhale like you've always been this cool. Be nineteen. Not nineteen in the scared way, but nineteen in the naive way. Ignore all consequences. When she says, *You should come see my apartment sometime,* don't hesitate to muster everything you've got and coolly reply, *How about right now?* Hold hands on the L train. When you giggle, she'll tuck her mouth to your ear and ask, *What?*, and you'll say, *Nothing.*

This may be because you are high, or it may be because you are finally, finally going home with a girl from the bar. A girl who is also named Courtney. Worry about that part later. Know that your friends will howl with jokes when you tell them this story tomorrow.

Enter her apartment like you're entering a museum: she has painted every surface with so many things, and now you want to hold your face up close to the whorls of paint and study it. Listen as she rummages in her bedroom, rolls another joint, and asks you what you think. Say, simply, *I like it.* Ignore when she puts Dave Matthews Band on the stereo. Seriously, just ignore it. From this day forward you will experience a strange weakness whenever you hear an acoustic version of "Crash Into Me," but it's okay, it will be the only casualty of this first time. Stay up until 2AM, or 3AM, or whatever AM it is, just talking, just feeling the warmth of her body next to yours as you sit on her twin bed, side by side. She will tell you that she is from Texas, and was raised to be a debutante, and even had a coming out ball. Then she will lean over you and dig into a plastic bin of papers and pull out a photograph, bent at the corner, and grin, holding it up for you to see. It's her, in a long pink gown, with long and wavy hair, holding a bouquet, face frozen in mild terror, a boy in a suit stiffly propping her up. Shout, *No way! No! Way!* Sitting here beside you, she is skinny, with dark eyes, and her shaved head, wearing black jeans with paint splattered on them, and a hoodie sweatshirt where the cuffs have worn to shreds. Her fingernails are dirty. She says she was sketching with charcoal earlier that day. Watch her smile shyly, tucking her head down. Lean forward. Kiss her. Kiss her now. Do not sleep. Know that the sun will come up, peeking through the dirty kitchen windows, visible just beyond her bedroom door, before you are done. Wonder if your roommate is curious that you never came home last night. Smile into the pillow when she begins to snore. Think, *The first girl I ever slept with had my same name.* Think, *that's how I'm going to begin this story when I get home.* At nineteen, it will all feel like stories, fast paced, raw, and unbelievable. Write it down.

You'll always like girls. You always did. In the sixth grade, you were so proud to have found the perfect Christmas gift for your best friend Lindsay Beck: a tiny love poem folded into a paper box. The love poem says that the box contains all the love you'll ever have for them. Grin, pleased, as she opens it. You will think it's sweet. She will think it's weird. In fact, the rest of the afternoon at her house, on this day when you were supposed to stay for dinner and exchange Christmas gifts (you couldn't wait, you had to give hers right then, as soon as you got off the bus), she will sit coldly on the other end of the couch and not look at you. Then before dinner, she will tell her mother she is not feeling well, and her mother will drive you home, without Lindsay, asking questions about your family and Christmas and did you get your tree yet? Mutter one-word answers. Stare blankly. You are confused.

This is just the first of many rejections, though. Girls can be mean. In school, they can be mean, and weird, and unreadable, and sometimes kind, and talkative, and think you're funny, and maybe eat lunch with you. Surround yourself with girls. Eventually, you will find the girls who like girls. It will not happen until the twelfth grade, and it will be Angela Giacchini, who shaved her head and donned a leather jacket long before you even knew what to call your attraction to girls, but one day in high school you will look out the window from the yellow school bus, and see her, boldly kissing her girlfriend, and you will think, like a bell in a church, *I want that.*

Do not be afraid of this moment. It's the beginning. Open up. Throw yourself into making art. Write for hours, and use charcoal pencils, and read the books at the library that you find when you nervously throw the word *lesbian* into the card catalogue system. (An even safer word, *bisexual*, has been introduced into your vocabulary, but "lesbian," you find, is a better search term in the Chester County Public Library.) Hide the books from your mother. Read them in the middle of the night. Read the scene in *Annie On My Mind* where Annie finally kisses Liza, and think, *Does that sound good? Does that sound like me?* Compare it to the thousands of boy-kisses-girl girl-kisses-boy stories you've seen and read and watched and heard over the years. You've got a lot to learn. Smile at Angela Giacchini in the vast hallways of your high school, even though you have not spoken to her since you sat at the same table group in Mrs. Carr's third grade class. When your mother discovers an overdue notice for *Queer Thirteen: Gay and Lesbian Writers Recall The Seventh Grade,* and asks you point blank if you have anything you'd like to tell her, stare dumbfounded at the kitchen linoleum as you pack your lunch in the morning and say, *No.*

Sit with Angela Giacchini during lunch. Wonder where she is when she's sick on Monday, and Tuesday, then Wednesday, and Thursday. Learn from your friend Jill who heard from Missy who's friends with Angela that her girlfriend dumped her for some punk kid named Dave. In eight years, Angela's ex-girlfriend and the punk kid Dave will get married, and Jill will be in the wedding and photos of it will crop up on Facebook, but that's not important right now. What's important is the day that Angela Giacchini returns to school, wilted and pale, you will drop your lunch bag across from her's in the cafeteria and say, *I'm so sorry.* She'll ask why, and you'll blurt out: that you heard that she was dumped, that it's so unfair, that heartbreak is awful, and you want her to know that you think she is really cool, and ask if she's heard the new PJ Harvey album yet and if you can make her a copy. She will scowl, taking this all in, before her face softens and she asks, *Who's PJ Harvey?* Tell her she is in for a fucking treat.

Holler that you're borrowing the car. Don't ask, just holler. Follow the directions Angela Giacchini has copied in the back of your Political Science notebook in her capital letter handwriting. Listen to The Breeders as loudly as the stereo in your mother's station wagon can go. Park the car. Put on chap stick in the rearview mirror, as if it is make up, which it is for you: a sheen of cherry flavored wax across your lips. Remember to breathe. This is just called hanging out. Right? Right. Ring the doorbell. Shake hands with her parents. Answer their questions about how your parents are and where you live now. Try not to notice how embarrassed Angela is, standing the doorway to the basement, where her bedroom is, where she is trying to lead you, so you can hang out. Give her the PJ Harvey CDs. Sit on the bed, because there is nowhere else to sit. Not everyone in life will have an Angela Giacchini. Not every queer teenager trapped in the suburbs before *Glee* or the It Gets Better campaign will have an Angela Giacchini. Grin at each other. Laugh nervously. Tell her to put on Rid of Me. Nod your head to the music. Relax. She doesn't even know you like girls. Not yet.

Weeks will go by, during which you will lend each other CDs, and talk on the phone, and eat lunch together, and watch lesbian foreign films that Angela special orders from a shop in the city, sitting on her bed, a bowl of popcorn gone cold between you. There will be something obvious between both of you, but it hasn't been said yet. Not until one night when you leave her house, and she walks you to the bottom of the driveway where you parked your mother's car. Here, you will stand outside, talking for another twenty minutes or so, even though it is February and your teeth are chattering. Wait until there is a pause. Watch her stuff her hands in her pockets and rock back on her feet. Say it now. Don't be awkward. Say, *I have a confession to make.* She'll knit her eyebrows together and tilt her head and ask you what kind of confession. Blurt it out: *I think like you. I know I like you. I've liked you for a while.* Watch her raise her head with a broad smile and ask, *Really?* Laugh and tell her, yes, really. Hold your breath. Stop holding your breath. Don't worry that your feet feel numb from standing in the cold this long. She'll move closer to you. You'll wait for seconds—minutes? days?—until she puts a hand on your neck, pulls you close, and kisses you.

Kiss her back. Kiss for a long time. Kiss until your glasses fog and you both can't stop laughing and it can't be February and feel this good. Kiss her again. Say goodnight. Get in your mother's car and watch her walk up the driveway to the warm light of her house. Whoop with joy as you drive home. Drum on the steering wheel. Shout, to no one in particular, over the volume of the radio, *She kissed me!* Drive around the quiet streets just to prolong the moment. Don't slam the door for once when you get home. Hum while you brush your teeth. Go to bed happy.

It won't last forever, this feeling, or Angela, who will start to date another girl, and then you'll move to New York, and then you'll lose touch with each other, even though you think of her a lot. But every time you like a girl, the feeling will return. On the second or third date, right before you kiss them for the first time, and right after you kiss them for the first time, on the subway ride home, or when you see it's her who is calling, or when she buzzes your apartment, when she waves from across the block—you will be a teenager again, driving home from Angela Giacchini's house, squealing with delight.

Like girls. Even when you don't get what you want. Even when your mother accuses you of just never having met the right guy. Even when you get called names. Even when the girls you like cheat on you, or turn out to have a drug problem, or own too many cats (six!), or break your heart, or stand you up, or yell at you in the street, or are indecisive, or haven't been with a woman before, or girls think you're too young, or never call you back. Wake up the next day and do it again. Believe that love exists. Live in a city where girls like girls. Smile. Go up to her and say hello.

Almost Touching, Almost Free

Dustin M. Hoffman
Western Michigan University, PhD

Suzie and Tofer are running away from home together. Not so much because they are in love but because it's easier to imagine lives run away in pairs. They are fifteen and fourteen, respectively. Tofer is younger, Suzie more in love. She imagines a twenty-seven-year-old Tofer, tall, bearded, more beautiful than he is now with his pocked jawline of acne. Tofer imagines a clean, empty apartment, without Tofu-To-Go bags rotting around the trashcan and piled on the oven, without exercise schedules and schematics glued to the carpet, an apartment where his ancient baby bouncy seat and stroller and crib aren't used to store unsold Tupperware.

Suzie and Tofer are running away and they are free. One mile and three-quarters and two miles and one-quarter from their homes, respectively. They jump the creek that divides the city of Kalamazoo between houses and plots of nothing where factories used to exist. Suzie jumps first. Tofer doesn't jump because he doesn't need to because the city has drained this creek. With the extinction of paper mills and beavers in the year 2042, creeks were deemed useless and converted to damp trenches. His sneakers squish into the loose loam, sink for a moment, and then they're free.

On the other side, Suzie breaks into a sprint, hoping Tofer is close behind. She knows boys like to chase. She's been chased by boys before, by Simon Winkler, Lance Duhadway, and Uncle Wallace. She hopes Tofer will notice the silver-studded belts around her waist bouncing in the night. These studs mean she is hard, like a thorn, like a brick of concrete, and Tofer will want to smash that concrete, jam his thumb against that thorn until he bleeds or the thorn snaps. Suzie also wears a low-cut tank top, no bra, and if Tofer catches up, he'll notice her soft parts, too, and will want to catch them, cup them in his hands, because that's what being in love is all about: the running and the catching and the cupping.

Tofer lags behind. He lets her run and thinks that running away can also be accomplished by walking. That's how he has lived for fourteen years—slow and solitary. Alone in his room, tapping his snare drum, a gift from his seventh grade band teacher, Mr. Freese, who was a good man but was fired anyway for smoking meth in the school parking lot. Tofer doesn't actually tap his snare. If he does, his parents bang on the wall, on his door, and eventually on his back if he doesn't stop. So, Tofer has made an art of almost hitting his drum, of coming within a millimeter of stick meeting head. Tofer plays the rhythm of silence as well as any fourteen-year-old ever played the rhythm of non-silence. Tofer's parents can't be disturbed; they are at work slimming down their souls. The healthy adult soul should weigh exactly forty-six grams. Scientists discovered that the soul is fattened by watching game shows and eating tomatoes and looking up, and this fat leads to a lack of logical capacity, fits of screaming, and an invisible, yet disgusting skin disorder called soul moles. Soul weight can only be reduced by performing exercises that are a cross between a half-lotus meditation pose and a kind of half-sit-up where one says "boof" at the peak of muscle contraction. Tofer's soul weighs seventeen grams and Suzie's weighs sixty-four. Doctors would diagnose her as suffering from soul obesity, if her parents cared about soul weight. They do not. They eat tomatoes every night, tape the newspaper to the ceiling and stare out their two-dozen skylights, their necks endlessly tilted. They live to spite a world gone soul crazy, live to ignore a thing they can't see and thus don't believe in.

Suzie despises her parents' soul neglect. Her parents keep her from the soul she deserves. She sprints across the open field, tumbles to the ground, pulls one foot over the other, and does a kind of half-sit-up. "Boof," she says. She hopes Tofer notices from wherever he is behind her. On her twelfth "boof" Tofer passes her, walking, wanting so badly to drown out her boofs with the sound of his fists pounding giant bass drums. Instead he almost-taps his jeans without making a noise because his hands stop a millimeter from impact.

Suzie hops up and follows, catches up to him. "Your soul is so slim," she guesses. "What's your secret?" This is something she's heard girls at school say, and this is something the girls at school have heard their older sisters say, and this is something the girls at school's older sisters have seen in the movies and TV, which is exactly what Suzie's parents are afraid of. In truth, no one can actually see anyone else's soul. This is scientific fact.

"I don't think I have one," Tofer says.

"I wish I could get rid of mine. It's so fucking fat, don't you think?" Suzie pulls the top of her tank top away from her sternum and points down at her breasts. This is not where the soul would be viewed if a soul could be viewed, but Suzie figures she has nice breasts so why not start there.

Tofer looks down her shirt, at her wonderful, braless breasts. He wants to almost-touch them. He wants to hover his fingers so close to her skin that it raises in goose bumps to meet him. "I think it's exactly as fat as it needs to be."

Suzie pulls Tofer close by the belt loops of his jeans, presses his crotch against hers. Tofer squirms backward, slightly. She kisses him, slides her tongue into his mouth, and inside Tofer's mouth his tongue retracts, hides against his lower teeth. Suzie's tongue stabs at the hidden lump, and it darts back farther. She rubs her tongue against the front of his teeth. She swabs her tongue against the thin flap of wet flesh that connects his tongue to the bottom of his mouth, and she thinks that the thinness of this bit of flesh probably has something to do with the thinness of Tofer's slim soul. She feels his dick hardening against her, pretends it's his soul swelling, and she feels less alone in the world of obese souls.

Suzie is only half-right about the physical body's correlation with soul weight. The tongue's frenulum linguae does indeed reflect the soul's density and stores sixty-two percent of its matter. The penis and its swelling contain exactly none of an individual's soul. Though Dr. Cianfrocco proved soul weight over a decade ago in 2029, the specific anatomy of the soul won't be discovered for another five years, until a scientist named Gertrude Cust renovates the super collider in Geneva to accommodate human cadavers. She will propel the cadavers at one mile per hour below the speed of light 5147 times. Cust's assistants will laugh at their flailing limbs, and then feel ashamed for laughing at the bodies so generously donated by the deceased. Eventually the bodies will smash into one another perfectly in a flash of luminous magenta, eviscerating all matter but the parts that contain the soul, which is primarily the frenulum linguae. And aren't the minds of adolescents like Suzie's wonderful things? The way they think about bodies—as they explore their own bodies and each other's bodies—can foretell the greatest discoveries. This has been happening since 4053 BC, but then and now and soon no one really listens. And Gertrude Cust will win her Nobel Prize in physics without the aid of Suzie, who will by then no longer be an adolescent, but will still remember the feel of that shy little scrap of wet flesh below Tofer's tongue.

Tofer will remember the terror in touching, of Suzie's fingers clutching his belt loops, and then descending to his dick which is hard and which he doesn't touch because his parents burst into his room two years ago to remind him of soul exercise time and found him touching himself. They told him that would ruin the fitness of his soul, which he doesn't care about, but shame lingers, and ever since he only dares to rub against the fabric of his jeans without using his hands. But now here are Suzie's hands, Suzie's lips on his, Suzie's tongue in his mouth.

Suzie stops exploring the thin strip of flesh under Tofer's tongue when a deep voice speaks. Suzie and Tofer part and peer into the dark field that used to contain factories and creeks. They see nothing, so Suzie says to the nothing, "What?"

The darkness replies, "You're too young to be going at it like that." And then a body emerges. A tall man, thin as a closed umbrella, who crinkles as he walks closer. He wears a white plastic bag on his head like a bonnet. His shirt is made of white plastic bags knotted together. His pants are also made of white plastic bags, ruffled layers, as if he stepped through three hundred of them. This is in fact what he did.

"How old do you think we are?" Suzie says. "Maybe we just look young to old people."

"You're too young to be dry-rubbing and tonguing and such."

"And what's the cutoff for something like that?"

"Look, little lady," the man says, "if you want an exact number, you're not going to get it. I'm retired from that game."

The man wearing the plastic bags is indeed retired from the game called The Mysterious Murray Guesses Your Age and Weight, which he used to perform at the carnival, back when there were still paper mills and beavers and before there was a scientific measurement for souls. Murray had an accuracy rating of ninety-two percent, the best in the age-weight-guessing business. But once souls became a factor, and carnival law required this weight to be itemized as a separate guess, Murray's accuracy dropped like a plastic bag full of bowling balls. He walked away from his previously successful career, unwilling to be mediocre at his craft. Age-guessing is a sore subject for Murray.

"Well, that's just fine, because I don't really give a fuck how old you think we are," Suzie says.

"Why are you wearing bags?" Tofer asks.

"That is a stupid question," Murray says. "Why aren't *you* wearing bags? Does your cotton repel water? Is your cotton completely free and found in nearly every trash bin you encounter? Does your cotton ward off evil and block microwaves and draw out sweat to extract toxins?"

"What does it do to soul weight?" Suzie picks up and examines a plastic bag Murray has shed.

Murray snatches the bag from her. "That is also a stupid question."

Suzie crosses her arms over her breasts, and feels her cheeks flushing. What Murray says echoes what her parents have said about soul weight: stupid. Someone somewhere must care about the dangerously high weight of her soul and how much better she could be if she was lighter.

"So, just sneaking out for a little tongue exploration," Murray says, "or running away from home?"

"How did you know we're running away?" Tofer says.

"Again, I'm retired from the guessing game, so stop asking me questions. If I'm right just confirm by nodding your head and maybe give me a dollar." Murray dives his hand inside the hundreds of plastic bags ruffling his legs and eventually comes up with the plastic bag designated for his wallet, which contains 354 cents in various coins. "Do you have a dollar?"

"We don't have any money," Suzie says, even though she has all the money she's ever had and all the money she managed to steal from her parents before she left. If she converted her bills into coins they would weigh twelve pounds and four ounces, or fifteen pounds and seven ounces, or eight pounds and zero ounces. All of these weights would tear a hole in Murray's bag-wallet, which is already stretched. Though it doesn't leak now, it would with Suzie's money, which he would convert to coins, because only coins can be melted down. Dollars can only be burned and are worthless if America's currency system rips apart.

"If you don't have money, you should come with me," Murray says. He turns away and starts walking.

Tofer follows. Suzie grabs his arm, tries to stop him, but Tofer shrugs her off. He does not know what to do with her touch, but he likes the swish-swish rhythm the bags make to Murray's stride. Tofer says, "Where else would we go tonight?"

So Suzie goes along, too. Goes because he goes, but not just because he goes. Murray's direction is the opposite from home.

The three of them trek across the great, sodded plains of the Eco-Take-Back project, which is just ten acres of sod slapped across ten acres that used to be paper mill ruins. The Eco-Take-Back project was seen as a great success, since grass is much more aesthetically pleasing than ruined brick. Murray stays in front, walking at a brisk crinkle. Tofer taps his hands to the rhythm of the crinkling without actually tapping anything. Suzie bides her time, cranes her neck, looking for something that will distract Tofer, something that will bring him back to her. There is nothing but sod. If she started digging, she'd find exactly what she needed: two brick shards she could clink primordially, like the first notes the Earth ever played with its grinding tectonic plates. But she doesn't dig. Her nails are freshly painted black and she would prefer to maintain the dark sheen rather than burrow, if the choice occurred to her, which it does not.

At the far edge of the Eco-Take-Back preserve, they traverse another empty creek and reach a row of huddled houses, dark and empty and boasting dangers on bright orange signs stapled to their front doors. Murray ignores these warnings, trudges toward a blue one-story with a mossy roof and a cracked bay window. He skips the front entrance and weaves through a broken fence. Tofer follows and so Suzie follows. At the back of the house, Murray drops to all fours and squeezes through a small window in the foundation.

His swish-swish bags crescendo in a great groan of crumpled plastic. And then he is gone.

Tofer drops to all fours, too. That screaming plastic music beckons him, but Suzie digs her heel into his pant leg.

"Why are we following this nut job?" she says. "He's probably going to rape the shit out of us."

"He's going to show us something," Tofer says.

"He's going to show us the tip of his dick before he shoves it in your mouth."

"How can we know unless we follow him?" Tofer yanks his pant leg free. "If you're scared, just go home to your family. You don't have to follow me."

What Tofer says causes Suzie to lose exactly 2.5 grams of her soul instantly. More soul excision than two weeks of doing 150 boofs per day. Rather than feeling slim, it feels like when her parents let Uncle Wallace take her to the Exploding Elbows' reunion show. The music through the speakers thumped so loud her chest rattled and he shared his beer with her and bought her a patch stitched with the band's name, and then he drove home with his dick sticking out the fly of his jeans. She looked out the passenger window the whole way home, at her face reflected there, Uncle Wallace's dick behind it.

The Uncle Wallace feeling sucks the will out of Suzie, and she lets Tofer slide into the basement window and disappear like Murray. She feels like disappearing, too, like there's no point to continuing on toward freedom and no way she can return home. Suzie lowers her palms to the dirt, digs her shiny fingernails into the grime, then slides through the window.

Suzie's feet touch ground, but she sees nothing. Inside is pitch black. Suzie hears Murray's crinkling, and something like tinny metal, and a squeaking. The noises and the darkness scare her and she reaches for Tofer and there he is. Her hand touches his small bicep, trailing down to his twitching wrist, his tapping hand, which she clutches, squeezing away those silent taps he's always doing. A nervous tick, she thinks.

Murray lights a lamp, a candle blazing inside a plastic milk jug. He raises it above his head and latches it to an eyehook hanging from a beam. Suzie spots stairs behind him, but the basement is cramped and Murray and his bags stand between her and escape.

"Kids, this is the gang," Murray says. "Gang, this is some kids."

"Howdy," one of them says. This one of them is Turkey. Tin foil covers his entire body, except for protruding pink toes. Only his toes and his mouth are uncovered, and two holes the width of a pencil where his nose should be, and two more for his eyes.

"And the other one is Pete." Murray points to a pile of Styrofoam. Big blocks of Styrofoam and small blocks teeter in one giant pile. The pile says nothing, does not move. Suzie doubts a man crouches or squats inside. She doubts anyone is there. Suzie does a lot of doubting in this basement of a vacant house with men she assumes are crazy, yet are most certainly free.

"Pete only moves in complete darkness, so you won't get much out of him. I see you doubting his existence, and that's bound to happen, but I assure you he is real and he is there."

Tofer examines the pile, estimates that a single man could fit perfectly inside. He imagines it is very quiet in there.

"How old are these two?" Turkey rises in a roar of twisting tin foil.

"This question never ends." Murray shakes his plastic bag-bonneted head.

"Old enough to know we shouldn't be hanging around you nut-jobs," Suzie says. She still clutches Tofer's hand and tugs it toward the window. The window appears tiny in the dim lighting, and sits so far above them. She wonders how they even found the floor without breaking their ankles. But this is the magic of the dark, of not seeing, and thus not wondering. It's the same combination of unknowns that allows Pete to exist without proof under his pile of Styrofoam blocks.

Pete existed the span of an adult life outside of Styrofoam blocks. He packaged and shipped industrial earplugs at a factory that roared all day long. He worked for forty-two years without any boss ever knowing his name. The earplug factory still tries to send him pension checks, but they don't have a name on file, can only find an address, and when they write him they get no reply since Pete is here or not here under a pile of Styrofoam and only moves in complete darkness.

Murray crinkles over to a metal shelf and removes a red gas can filled with whiskey. He takes five Styrofoam cups from the pile, asks Pete, "Do you mind if I use these?"

The pile of Styrofoam doesn't answer.

Murray pours a little whiskey into each cup, then passes them around to Suzie, Tofer, and Turkey. He downs his own. He lifts the last one toward Pete, holds it in the air, swirls it, waits. Finally he sets it on the pile of Styrofoam.

Suzie looks inside her cup and studies brown stains above the rim of brown liquid. She has drunk alcohol before, knows she's too young, but her parents find age restrictions as absurd as ideal soul weight. She drinks, wishes someone cared. Tofer clenches his cup, accidentally digs a fingernail into the Styrofoam and makes a squeaking sound. He holds his breath, waits for someone to be furious, and when no one is he smiles.

"These kids have come seeking answers to their questions," Murray says. "Questions like how old are they and how much do they weigh, souls included, and what will they be when they grow up, and when will they die, and how will it happen."

"We don't care about that," Suzie says. "We never asked you those things."

"Not directly, my dear," Murray says, "not directly."

"Are we counting previous lives?" Turkey asks. Turkey worked at the carnival with Murray and read Tarot cards and crystal balls or customers' palms or sometimes just their general auras, which Turkey can smell. One whiff and he can tell Tofer's soul has lived five hundred years, eighty-nine lives, fourteen of them very brief stints as a beetle, an earthworm, a bloodworm, a moth, and a now-extinct mammoth tick. When Tofer was a mosquito he lived only twenty-seven minutes. That part of his soul is still very disappointed at not getting a fair shot, never even sucking a drop of blood. Tofer the mosquito froze to death because its neglectful mother laid eggs in late November.

"No, we are not counting previous lives," Murray says.

"This is pointless," Suzie says. "Let's get out of here."

Tofer squeaks his fingernail across his cup.

Pete understands what Tofer means. He scratches a toenail against the inside of his cave. He would like to invite Tofer to come live with him in the safety of Styrofoam, where all sound is protected and swaddled and even the most minor almost-tap of fingertips reverberates, sways electrons, makes a fine tinkling sound.

Turkey tips up his cup, throws it to the floor, stomps upon it. "To reveal these answers, a reading is absolutely in order. To the roof!"

Turkey jogs up the stairs in a great chiming of crunching metal. Murray crinkles up after him. Suzie turns and jumps at the window, but can't reach it. There is nothing in the room for her to stand on. The Styrofoam, she knows, would snap under her weight, which she overestimates when factoring her obese soul. She shakes her head, spits out a "Fuck," and then trudges up the stairs, hoping for a door through which they could slip and get away from these people and be on their way to freedom again.

Before leaving the basement, Tofer balances his still-full cup of whiskey on Pete's pile, rests his hand on a large piece of Styrofoam, and asks, "Are you coming, too?"

Pete wants to tell him no, wants so badly to unbury his right hand and place it upon Tofer's. But the world outside Styrofoam is too harsh, too loud, like the bellowing factory floor, the roar of everything at once which sounds like madness. Pete's soul weighs .00786 grams, and could disappear in one bang. So he does nothing but let his heart thump, which he can hear perfectly in his

Styrofoam nest, a rhythm Tofer would love if he were in there, and their respective heartbeats could thu-thump together, playing off each other, a percussive two-man, two-heart, four-ventricle symphony of whomps and gurgles. But Tofer is gone, up the stairs, following the others, and Pete's heartbeats slow. Thump. Only four more left. Thump. What a wonderful thing to be alive and hear it so clearly. Thump. The blood swooshes an accompaniment. Thump. So quiet you can hear nothing.

Suzie clomps up the basement stairs. She reaches a giant hall where Turkey and Murray are thundering up parallel staircases that hug each wall. She walks up the right side. From there an iron staircase spirals up to a tiny platform holding a stepladder, which she climbs, until her head smacks a ceiling access panel. She no longer knows if Tofer follows. She only knows up is the only direction left. So she lifts the panel, and there is the night sky hanging heavy and present above the roof's sparkling shingles.

She walks to the roof edge, feeling alone. But she also feels free, so far above the home she left behind, until she looks over the eave and sees the ground only twelve feet below.

Tofer's hand taps the air at her side. "We could jump," she says. "It would hardly hurt."

"Or you could watch as we reveal your fortunes," Turkey says, rattling between the two. He carries a white sink basin and heaves it over the edge. The shards explode on the concrete. Turkey rubs his tin foil chin, studies the shards. "Inconclusive. We're going to need more porcelain."

So Murray brings a toilet, missing its tank, and heaves that over, too. "More, more," Turkey says, wringing his wrists, crumpling the foil until his arms become tiny sticks. And Murray brings the missing tank and heaves it and Turkey calls for more and more.

Murray and Turkey take turns hurling more sinks and toilets. When Suzie is sure they've exhausted their supply, they break out naked dolls, cat figurines, and sculptures of praying hands.

"They're from the carnival days," Murray explains. "You would have won a cat or porcupine if I'd been wrong about your weight, the praying hands if I'd misjudged your age. Or a comb or a harmonica or a screen-printed Scorpions collector mirror, but we ran out of those long ago. The dolls were a little harder to earn." Murray tosses three more praying hands, and then Turkey yells, "Stop," and Murray throws another.

"For Christ's sake, Murray," Turkey leans over the eave, studies the porcelain-littered concrete, "you've overdone it. You're a child of excess just like the rest of them. Now we'll need more."

So the two men chuck twenty-two more porcelain knick-knacks until Turkey is satisfied and has worried his fingers thin as pencils.

"Now it's perfect," he says. "Just look at that."

Suzie and Tofer look, and they see a street of white shards. Like dinosaur bones, Tofer thinks. Like a brontosaurus exploded, Suzie imagines. Like a pterodactyl exhibit that got the shit shaken out of it, Murray conclusively conceives.

"It's like looking into the future, right?" Turkey says.

And no one agrees to this, but that doesn't bother Turkey. He reads the shards, sums it up in his head. He sees a Cro-Magnon's quarter skull-case, and that means the dead will rise again. He sees a toilet plunger, and that means the return of lost desires. He sees a boat anchor for a three-quarter size sailboat, and that means lost travelers will hesitate. He sees a half-full Styrofoam cup, and he knows that Pete is dead. He sees a candy apple and he sees oak leaves and he sees a tire iron and he sees Jacques Cousteau and he sees a lasso, and these things mean something, but he doesn't explain any of that to Tofer and Suzie. He peers over the edge, waiting to start like an arcade game waiting for its nickel.

"We'll need two carnival tickets now," Murray says.

"Two what?" Tofer says.

"He won't read a fortune unless you give him two tickets. Routine is hard to break, children."

"Why would we have carnival tickets?" Suzie says.

"Or you could just tell him you're giving him carnival tickets and give him a hundred dollars or twelve cereal box tops or the promise of your first born son. He won't know the difference."

"Or we could just leave," Suzie says.

"That is impossible," Murray says. "We've already started, and what's started can't be stopped. I mean, what would we do with all that porcelain? It doesn't glue itself back together. Hell's bells, you could have just told us from the start that you didn't have any tickets."

Turkey looks worried. He rubs his now crumpled fist into his eyeholes, leaving dents in the foil. He crosses and uncrosses his legs, which grow thinner and thinner. There will be nothing left of Turkey if they don't do something to appease his need for carnival tickets. Tofer understands. Tofer understands needing something to the point of silence, of disappearing. He near-taps his hips, imagines the impact, and where he usually envisions contact and sound, now gaping holes have replaced his thighs. His fingers have become rogue black holes that would eat through his body if they came close. Contact is a millimeter away and also nowhere.

"Tickets please," Turkey says, poking at them with his thin fingers-claws. "Tickets please oh please oh please."

And then Turkey drops to the shingles, wraps his arms around his knees in a fetal position. He hugs himself until he becomes a giant ball of tin foil.

"Well, now you've done it," Murray says. "It's going to take days to unfold him."

"I think we better go," Suzie says.

"You think?" Murray pulls up his plastic bag sleeves, and underneath is more plastic. He closes in on Suzie, towers over her. "Who asks to get their fortune told and isn't prepared to pay for it? What kind of patrons are you?"

"We didn't ask for shit, asshole." Suzie pushes Murray's chest, and a few bags flutter to her feet. He scrambles to gather them up, and Suzie slips one into her tank top.

Tofer watches and worries, near-taps his hips faster. Murray reminds him of his father before Tofter went silent, when Tofer used to waste the day tapping pencils against cardboard and tire pressure gauges against buckets and his fingers against a pocket full of nickels and pennies. Murray glowers down at Suzie, who rolls her eyes, and that makes Murray's eyes squint harder. Tofer could fight this man, shove him off the peak and let him tumble upon porcelain shards. This is what he should do, to be a man, to protect his girl, to make contact, to make sound.

But Tofer does something much meeker. He grabs Suzie's hand, yanks her away, and he runs to the other edge of the roof and jumps. They fall. They fall and the earth approaches, but they have plenty of time to enjoy the push of the wind, the drop in their guts, weightlessness and also dropping as fast as porcelain praying hands. They fall and fall, passing the first-floor bay window, and they hear Turkey begging for tickets so that he won't disappear. They fall and fall, and when they look up, there is Murray waving, saluting, winking, saying, "Attaboy, attagirl, only one real path toward freedom. Imminent death for all and to all a good night." They fall and fall, and there goes the basement window, where they get a peek of total darkness, but even in total darkness a sliver of light reflects, a fractional percentage of .000493, and that's enough to see the Styrofoam pile shudder and then tumble, and the nothing inside revealed, the lack of body, a ballooning soul that is invisible.

They keep falling, and they keep holding hands. The ground is closer, but it never comes. They will shatter to pieces like so much porcelain before them. And Tofer has made peace with that. He'll make impact in a brilliant slap of flesh on concrete. It will be loud and heartbreaking and completely beautiful. His millennium-old soul will rise again, and perhaps become a creature who makes sound. Maybe a spruce pine growing wild from a trench that used to be a creek, and his branches will slap the neighboring houses crammed around him. Then he'll be chopped down, stripped of bark, sliced, and manufactured into pair of drumsticks.

But Suzie has a parachute. She pulls Murray's bag from her tank top, wraps her legs around Tofer's waist. She raises it above her head, where it catches wind, rips at her arms, her grip, but she holds tight, and Tofer and Suzie float.

The sum total of their souls is now ninety-eight grams. They night has slimmed Suzie, stretched Tofer. They float and enjoy the feeling of ninety-eight grams, which is the perfect weight for two souls together, on the run.

They land on the sidewalk under a lamppost that seems burned out but will relight in twenty-three seconds, as it has almost been five minutes and forty-four seconds—the exact amount of time a young Gertrude Cust discovered it could be dark on a street before ex-carnival worker squatters start moving into abandoned houses. This is what Gertrude Cust thinks she has proven. Later, at the end of her life, when she has become a recluse at the once-again abandoned collider, she will prove the existence of Pete, the greater importance of soul volume over weight. No one will publish the findings.

Suzie releases Tofer, and he near-taps his thighs. Tofer moves toward Suzie keeping his head down. He's afraid his lips and tongue will be required again and he won't know what to do. Suzie doesn't kiss him. She presses her hips against his. She grips his wrists and shifts his tapping fingers to her thighs, which are wider than his, exactly wide enough so that Tofer's fingers touch and make a soft sound. The lamppost flicks on. Tofer taps on Suzie, and the sound echoes toward their homes, two miles and one-quarter and two miles and three-quarters away, respectively.

Scraping

Louise Ells
Angila Rusking University, PhD

Everyone else has moved to the other side of the boat to photograph the porpoises following us out of the harbor. I can't let go of the rail; gripping it feels like the best way to ward off the sick I can already taste in the back of my throat. Not a boat person, never a boat person—that was a love my mother and brother shared.

I take shallow breaths through my mouth in an attempt to avoid the smell of engine exhaust and seaweed and the tub of dead fish for the puffins, and stare back at the Nova Scotia shoreline we've left, the wind farm on the horizon. I can see Dad shaking his head, hear him telling me to take deep breaths, focus on the horizon, look towards our destination, North Brother island, which is only a couple of miles off the starboard bow.

But that island is too flat to see and this isn't a direct journey. A man from Parks Canada will meet this boat of puffin watchers when it reaches its destination, over an hour away, and we'll retrace this passage back to the Brothers. It was the best I could manage to organize. It will be worth it, I promise myself, lousy as I feel, seeing the Roseate Terns was so high on Dad's wish list.

"Well, well," he said when he first read about it. It must have been in the quarterly newsletter he got detailing species sightings across the country. I remember the crinkly paper, pale blue, and my excitement every time I saw it our mailbox. I subscribe to online magazines now, and blog feeds, and mourn the passage of that era when mail brought pleasure. "Well, well. I grew up not thirty miles from the country's largest colony of Roseate Terns and had no idea. I'd very much like to go and see them, hear them." That would have been ten years ago, I was in my fourth year, home for Thanksgiving. Mum decided it was coffee time and the three of us spent the next two hours looking at maps and books, planning how to get there, stops along the way, then researching the birds. The Hummingbirds of the sea Audubon had called them.

We all knew it was a fantasy but Dad and I refused to acknowledge the reality out loud. "June," he said. "We'll go in June for the hatchlings." He kept a notebook in which he detailed plans for future birding excursions, and in his precise handwriting he filled in three pages for our Roseate Tern trip.

The deckhand does double duty as our tour guide, his voice crackling over an old PA system, giving a brief history of the geology of the islands we're passing, basic information about puffins, telling us to look out for harbor seals. Two young girls and their father cross the deck and stand next to me at the railing, the girls' excited chatter punctuated with *likes* and *you-knows*. "Like, and then she said, like—So I like—And after she like—we, like, you know." They soon lose interest in the view of the scrubby forest and wind turbines and go off in search of something, like, more exciting, leaving only their father and me.

I look at him—he's roughly my age, he looks as ill as I feel—then at his hands, which are holding tight to the rail. Farmers' hands with big fingers, rough skin, short nails. A kink in the baby finger on his left hand. Like Dad's. I look back at his face.

A bad habit of mine, staring at strangers. Staring, and wondering. Could this man be Daniel? I've noticed recently that the farther I am from home, the more I do it, when the possibility is even less plausible. In the obvious places I don't scrutinize each face I see for signs of resemblance. It only now occurs to me that he might have shown up at the funeral and I wonder if I would have seen him in the crowds. If I would have known.

I look at this man's profile again and he makes eye contact.

"Rough," he says, dipping his chin towards the whitecaps.

I nod. This is the tail end of a storm, which wound its way up from the Caribbean and ours is the first trip out in ten days. I assumed the Captain was joking when he told us to get ready for fifteen-foot waves. Apparently not. I could have paid more attention to the weather report, but this is the right week to come. This was the original plan. The eggs, laid in late May, will now be hatching. Two, most likely, though chances are only one will survive. That will be considered a breeding success, if one baby survives to become a fledgling.

There's an entire chapter in Dad's book devoted to common ornithological terms. Semi-precocial, pullus, fledgling—last night at the bed and breakfast, a farmhouse with a wraparound porch and flaking white paint—I chanted them from a to z, mentally ticking all the ones that apply to today's terns. I can feel the book in my pocket, the binoculars around my neck tucked inside my coat squishing it to my chest. As a child I loved checking off the birds I'd seen, keeping lists from the Christmas Day count, the summer holidays, our canoe trips. And I loved most of all the pre-dawn walks with Dad when we met other birders with Dad's book in their hands. I embarrassed him, always, when I told them he'd sign it for them. For three decades his was considered to be one of the definitive guides to birds of northeastern Ontario, right up there with Peterson and Sibley, but he was my hero, always.

"Bird watcher?" my rail mate guesses. "Here for the puffins?"

"Terns," I say. And at his blank look, "Like seagulls." Which is almost true. Families Sternidae and Laridae are closely related.

That makes him smile. "You're enduring all this for some shit-hawks? Hope it's worth the trip."

It will be. This had been my idea, when I asked Dad what he wanted and his answer had been vague. "Well. The Roseate Terns," I'd said. I'd found his notebook with the plans we'd made that long ago fall day and read them out to him. Things have changed since then, not least the designation of protected areas, but Dad's name still carries weight in the birding world so here we are, on our way to North Brother Island.

A big wave. The boat lifts and slaps down onto the sea, making the girls' father gag and lower his head over the rail.

It's possible. That's the thing. It's always possible. When I can't sleep I watch family dramas where a shift in the music signals a quarter of an hour until the credits. Just long enough for two estranged siblings, sisters most likely, to meet in some extraordinary place and explain, forgive, reunite. A collage of snapshots showing them as they were in the past and as they will be in the future. All forgiven. Best friends again.

I know how it goes. I also know that if I am ever to see my brother again it's unlikely to be on a boat tour off the coast of Nova Scotia. And this man is not my brother. Little as he ever cared about our father's hobby—Daniel called it an obsession—he would never refer to gulls as shit-hawks.

I have imagined moments, conversations; envisioned how it might feel to offer an olive branch. I've practiced a smile. I wonder if I'd turn and walk away, as he did the last time I saw him, in the local grocery store, pushing a full cart, which he abandoned in the dried goods aisle. I didn't even manage a hello because he'd spotted me first. It was late Saturday afternoon before Canadian Thanksgiving on Monday. I looked into his cart but there were no clues about his life, just a turkey, cranberries, tinned pumpkin. Exactly what you'd expect, exactly what I was buying.

Later, days later, I realized the kind thing to do would have been to buy my brother's groceries and have someone deliver them to him, someone who knew where he was staying. (Shops in our hometown still close on Sunday so he would have gone without the traditional meal.) But I didn't think of that in time, instead I paid for my shopping, drove to my parents' house, and made the sage and onion stuffing and the pumpkin pie and the maple-glazed squash for my mother's last Thanksgiving meal. I chopped a lot of onions to explain away my tears and debated with myself if it would be kinder to report the sighting or not. I wondered who he was visiting, what friends of his remained, what sort of person could see his sister and walk away like that, not visit his dying mother. In the end I said nothing. I couldn't stand the thought of the hurt in my mother's eyes.

The doctors had named the disease, explained why parts of her atria were no longer working as they should, but I knew better. More than one ornithologist has suggested that the birds who mate for life, turtledoves, swans, snow geese, can also die of a broken heart if they lose a child. The deck hand's commentary continues: leatherback turtles, whales, the cod fishing industry. A mention of my pink-breasted terns, their distinctive two-note call, the likelihood of only one of the two babies surviving to adulthood. They are accustomed to a certain amount of loss, he says, as if he knows this, as if he's spoken to the birds and they've reassured him, it's all right, we're accustomed to this.

I turn to the man at my side and start to tell him more. Roseates are an old species, I explain. They breed in colonies close to, but estranged from other terns. They take, or are given, the less favourable nesting areas and create a scrape in the sand or gravel, which they cushion with softer reeds and grasses. His daughters interrupt us, rushing back in mid-argument about whose turn it is to use the camera. He mediates, sends them off, shrugs at me. "Siblings."

I thought it might be one good thing I could do for Dad, finding Daniel. For myself, I wasn't sure that seeing him again would restore the part of me I'd lost when he left. The days of skating on the river in winter, summer camping holidays, secrets in our treehouse—all so long ago. And farther back, the nights we'd snuggled on the sofa to listen to Dad's bedtime stories which always started the same way: "When I was a little boy in Nova Scotia." Until we could recite them, word for word, and I had a clear picture in my mind of the boy who bullied him in fifth grade, the one Dad had raced and beaten to the forest for the best Christmas tree. The smell of the hogs his parents raised, the taste of his mother's Apple Brown Betty. The vignettes from Dad's childhood had been one of the anchors in mine. Ours.

My brother had made clear his choice. I wrote to him, two letters, years apart, both returned with a 'not at this address' message, scribbled over the front of one, stamped over the other. His handwriting, perhaps, or that of a new tenant in the apartment building, new home owner? I didn't know if it was true, no longer at this address, or his way of declaring that nothing had changed. As stubborn and as proud as he'd always been. So like our mother. No contact, no contact ever was the last thing he'd yelled at me the day he left.

Last year I tried online, typing his name into Google, LinkedIn, Facebook and several of those websites that promise to find anyone anywhere, *for the low low price of*. I paid. I read random obits in case he'd predeceased us both. I called his childhood friends. It was only when I seriously considered hiring a private investigator that I told myself I had to stop searching. For Daniel, for the real reason he'd left the family, for any hope of ever understanding. Instead I gathered maps and books and sat with Dad and planned holidays for the two of us.

The puffin island comes into sight and there's the Parks Canada man waiting in a Boston whaler. I thank the Captain, say goodbye to the girls' father, and make my way across the gunwale of the big boat and clamber down into the shallow dinghy.

Once we've set off, I raise Dad's binoculars to my eyes, scanning the sky, focusing in on the birds that are catching the wind and diving for fish. Black Guillemots, Great Black-backed Gulls, Eiders, and, of course, my Terns. Their long tail feathers and blush pink breeding colours as elegant as Audubon promised. As we near the rocky shore the Parks Canada man cuts the motor and points out the scrapes where the eggs and days-old hatchlings are.

We left the doctor's office, the same doctor who'd given us the best-case scenario of three months for Mum, in January, in silence. In the parking lot I'd panicked. "I can't lose you too, I can't let go. I don't know how to." I had clung to my Dad's arm like a child and added, selfishly, it's not fair, I can't do this again, you can't leave me alone.

Dad had patted my hand, held it, tight against his arm. "You'll be okay Daisy-girl," he'd said, using a nickname I'd not heard in years. "You know how to cope. You'll figure out what to do." That was the evening I found his notes about this trip, read them aloud to him, got down the same maps and books we'd looked at with Mum.

I don't believe the deckhand's version is correct. I don't believe a tern is accustomed to a certain amount of loss. She must hope, every year when she lays two eggs, she must think: maybe this is the year both my children will thrive.

I take the mulberry bark urn from my inside pocket where it's nestled against Dad's book, and lean over the edge of the whaler, holding it close to the water, opening one end. I've been warned this won't be romantic, a gentle breeze won't pick up the ash and carry some of it to the heavens, sprinkling the rest on the surface of the sea, sparkling in a ray of sunshine which breaks through a grey cloud, illuminating a clear path ahead. But this eco-friendly thing is supposed to help the process, then float for a few moments before gracefully submerging.

There is none of that. A stickiness and a sinking and then a wave snatches it, paper and bag and all, leaving only a dark smudge on my hand which is rinsed away by the next wave. The poem I start to recite is drowned out by the harsh call of a tern. A few feet away there is a reply from another.

Peaceful Village

Jane Summer
Goddard College, MFA

B endt was the black dog of the neighborhood—overweight, overgrown and over-mean for a kid his age. There was something of the beast about him and like a beast Bendt was always on the prowl for someone to push around and take a bite of. At the hint of him—the massive belly sloshing with snails and rusty nails, *fee-fi-fo-fum* footsteps, darkening downy lip—flanked by his pimpled, twin-redhead bodyguards, kids flew away like buckshot. Except the once.

The kids on my street, all about three years one side of ten, claimed the woods. More a fallow field now that the last farmer had moved on, it was our secluded playland. Bound at a right angle by two paved arteries and on its other two sides by our neighborhood streets, the field echoed with the twang of far-off traffic, punctuated with the occasional scream of a chainsaw or the grunt of a bulldozer. My next-door neighbor Clarissa might be right about it being haunted here. Farmers don't like watching their land shrink before their eyes, like a piece of cherry pie bitten down by grownups until dessert's not worth getting excited about.

House builders, like gravediggers, broke earth. Without pause. Along my street, backyard boundary markers—straight-back fences, flat-face stones, prickly hedges—went up fast, and flanked the mallowy field's perimeter. Gateway to the field was best found on our property. By climbing through the split-rail fencing in my backyard, an untended area reckless with wild blueberry bushes, apple blossoms, buttercups, butterflies, bumblebees, and crickets, kids from the neighborhood gained furtive access to the woods. My brother Joachim and I knew our backyard as a proto-woods, though when we first moved in the yard had been hoed and sodded just like all the submissive yards in the development. Viewed from the street, however, our house was as its neighbors: the front lawn a thick emerald shag with a dandelion or two.

Bendt lived diagonally across the woods from Joachim and me in a house that, like most houses, gave nothing away: no holiday decorations, window blinds drawn, grass clipped, gray aluminum siding in good repair. A three-foot tall holly hedge surrounded the property. To access the field from his house Bendt shoved his body through his family's hedge, busting branches time and again until there was a sad furrow in the shrubbery—a herd of deer having a munch, his parents might have thought. Most often Bendt was with the twins and with the twins he entered from the highway because the redheads' fair skin reacted poorly to the scratches of the greenery. Entering off the highway at the north end of the field required an idiotically hazardous rock scaling, but Bendt ruled by bossing his gang. Eugene, our leader and our founder, liked to put things to the vote.

Eugene was older than everyone, must've been five or six grades ahead of me; Bendt just a grade ahead, but he'd been left back. Left back no one knew how many times. Where Eugene strode through the field, Bendt lumbered. Mud and grit complexioned Bendt's moon face; Eugene's skin was pale as an alabaster Jesus, a natural rose patina at the cheekbones. Bendt repelled folks like a full diaper; Eugene I admit didn't make much of an impression. People wanted to like him but there was something on a high shelf about him. His basketball coach was his most vocal supporter until Eugene's father roared the sunny fellow out the front door.

Eugene originally built a fort in the field with a lookout eight feet off the ground in an oak. He built it by himself. After a couple of kids and I encountered him at the thirty-eighth parallel with his evergreen rifle, the fort subsided into a peaceful village where everyone could play a part. Kids staked homes, delineated by twigs and stones, though one or two houses were simple cardboard refrigerator boxes, naturally air conditioned in summer. We developed our own currency consisting of ceramic and porcelain shards, which had ended up in the lot when developers dumped bathroom fixtures and tiles that had been damaged beyond repair during the installation of bathrooms, perhaps from my house, perhaps Eugene's, even Bendt's. In winter we built igloos so blue and solid you could stand atop them and be Admiral Peary for the day.

Rules were necessary. The first stated no objects—particularly the black, gold and lavender shards comprising our currency—were to be brought out of, or into, the village. The rule meant even Eugene, aboriginal villager and thus our *de facto* leader, was barred from importing his bow and arrow, long and tensile as his own body. No dolls, blankets, roll caps, or water pistols. Another rule allowed marriage between any two kids—whether siblings like Joachim and me, girlfriends, or two boys—as long as someone was the husband, someone the wife. Everyone in the village pulled water from the creek, as well as tadpoles and toads, but no one was to visit there unaccompanied, as the stream was dangerous territory, being situated halfway between Bendt's land and ours. Finally, whatever job we wanted was ours but it would be great if not everyone was the village cook, who flavored stews with onion grass and berries, which we were certain were highly poisonous.

We didn't speak of the woods to our parents or anyone outside our circle. We were afraid the authorities would raze our high weeds. It was the beginning of honorable lying. A transient exercised his unfriendly mongrel in our wooded village. Joachim spied him when home with the mumps and then the flu. Crooks "lost" strangulated stoolies and other unwanteds in our woods, though we never found a body. They didn't worry us. They might be amazed at our metropolis but they wouldn't squawk. They were compromised by their sins.

In reality we had only one predator.

Eugene engineered booby-traps around the perimeter of the village with pits deeply dug, having found a WWII trench shovel. (Clarissa, the second oldest community member, convinced everyone it bore splatters of dried blood). Knitted leaves and fronds of weeds concealed the traps.

"Do you think this is necessary?"

"No one says you have to help, Hanna." Clarissa had a way of meaning the opposite of what she was saying.

"Booby-traps are better than battle." If Eugene's father could hear him sounding like Gandhi, I said to Joachim.

Though I knew gathering grass made me a traitor to myself, I gathered grass. I was for the idea of wanting to protect the village, but the meanness of traps got under my skin and tugged.

Bendt, his house two school bus stops from the more closely clustered rest of us, was out of his jurisdiction when he broached our wooded village. Nevertheless, every season we could rely on him and his Tweedledees to come thrashing through the tall dry grass. He'd plop his book bag and clarinet on the curb where he exited the school bus and chase his target of the day, who'd try to make it home before Bendt collapsed on top of the kid. If the kid escaped, Bendt sought trouble in the woods. If Eugene were present the goons would scare. Otherwise, we villagers scattered and had to rebuild. Bendt always kicked the village to smithereens.

Summer closed down as it always does, school opened up stinking of new: new waxed floors, new melamine desktops, new pencils, new teachers. And a new village. One of Eugene's nine siblings announced Eugene wouldn't join us in the village again. His father squeezed him into Blessed Sacrament, which meant a twenty-minute drive and a ton of homework. When the kids grumbled, his brother reminded us no one argues with their 400-pound scalpel-wielding father, who'd just sacrificed his son to the church.

The image of Eugene in a black dress and beanie was harder to picture than his father in a tutu. My imagination had to suffice because in the only clear memory I had of Eugene after that last summer, he was getting into the parochial school carpool in his maroon sweater and gray slacks. It was colder than usual for fall, yet Eugene wore no coat. Before bending his lean frame into the station wagon, he paused at the top of the crest then turned in the direction of the woods, down the hill. I watched him from our front door, as I was about to leave for school. Eugene saluted, then folded himself into the car. Maybe he was just shielding his eyes from the sun but whatever was he was thinking, it seemed an intimate moment; something not meant to be witnessed.

I saw him a few times again, after dusk, in that anxious hour, when he played two-on-two with Joachim and others at the net under the streetlight in front of our house. Kids practiced squeaky trumpet, violin, and flute as night yawned its dark dog breath down our street. Any minute the surgeon's ugly black Fairlane would make its broad swoop around the corner, catching Eugene mid jump shot and summoning him into the auto.

Maybe we didn't see much of Eugene but his name rumbled from his house down the treacherous hill. His father—that trapezoid on stubs—hollered day and night, "Eu-GENE! Eu-GENE!" Everyone knew when Eugene's name echoed out over their roofs, the surgeon who put the black rubber mask over so many of our faces and slashed at our tonsils, adenoids, appendixes, was giving his eldest son the belt. With all that hollering, one day the man who pleasured in knifing folks would have himself a coronary. In the meantime, Eugene remained the kind of boy who'd take the blame for whatever trouble his eight siblings whipped up and whatever perversion the surgeon hadn't relieved himself of with one of his etherized patients. As for us motley villagers, we were fairly defenseless without Eugene, even given Clarissa, our self-appointed sorcerer. Despite her spells, potions, and hypnotisms, she ended up making us afraid of everything in the dark. But in the sun, we acted good pilgrims and knights, built dugouts and lookouts, and we sent smoke signals in case there were allies in the unknown world.

Labor Day having come and gone, the after-school hours in the village shrank fast. We shot out of the school bus to walk our dogs and finish homework in order to drag light from those brief, sun-stained hours. Bendt dropped his book bag and clarinet case at the bus stop to chase down a puny kid while those of us who built the village in the woods gathered crops of thistle and Queen Anne's lace before the first frost.

We were pitching crab apples at the flaming sky when Clarissa heard the rustling. Once it was a copperhead Eugene scared off by heaving a fractured Ming Green toilet lid in its direction. I wouldn't return to the woods for weeks after that, and then only when Joachim and Eugene hacked down the high grass in my path. Usually, the noises turned out to be sweet things—rabbits, field mice, a litter of kittens—and when anyone voiced interest in kill or capture I quickly drafted forbidding rules. But this time the clapping of reeds was exactly what we villagers most feared.

Bendt and his gang of two rose up without announcement. By the time anyone had seen them it was too late to run. "Don't come here!" Clarissa, now in command, shouted. "We have a gun."

We kids were aghast, especially Clarissa's sister, pretty little but high-strung Alma. I thought she was going to cry. Why would Clarissa say such a thing? Nobody ever brought anything from home into the village, not even a tomato sandwich, let alone a gun.

"They have a gun," Bendt laughed.

Hissing between her teeth, Clarissa ordered Joachim and me to get our stepfather's shotgun. Immediately.

"I'll shoot it if I have to."

"Oh yeah?"

"Yeah!"

"Let's see your gun."

The shotgun seemed nothing more than a tasteless ornament to Joachim and me, much like Eugene's brass bedside crucifix. We had never touched the Remington, which our stepfather used with terrible success at spring turkey hunts. But apparently Clarissa's eyes had been magnetized by the gun, as they'd been by the half-naked Indonesian dancer hung in stone above it. There was nothing like that in Clarissa's house. Only a thickly painted dancing rabbi and what looked to me like a pair of tombstones glued together. Everything struck Clarissa as art, while in Eugene's mind the dark crucifix above his bed was neither art nor symbol but simply there, like the basketball net or the fork his sister set at his dinner place.

"*Go!*" Clarissa snarled.

"I'm getting Eugene." One of his brothers, a pipsqueak replica of the soon-to-be Jesuit monk, crept away.

Joachim and I couldn't budge the gun. It was dead weight, like the iron barbell at Eugene's basement carnival. *Try your luck! A nickel a chance! Raise it off the ground and win all the simoleons in the pretzel jar!* My brother and I tried again, this time dragging the deadly thing out by its leather strap. Ku-lunk! Our eyes locked at the double-barrel hitting the Indonesian bas-relief above our stepfather's night table. But this was no time for art, and Joachim hefted the stock, I took the cold metal barrel and as if hauling quarry stones we stumbled our way back into the field of imagined forts and farmland and good marriages.

Clarissa took possession of the bolt handle and trigger and calm settled over the village inhabitants certain Bendt would retreat. He had to. We had a gun.

But Bendt didn't run. For a moment I thought everything would turn out all right, we'd shake on it, call a truce, walk away without fearing Bendt in the woods again. As I waited for the acquiescent handshake the sun picked out a lock of Alma's hair and turned it white as vanilla ice cream. Squinting in the brightness, Alma grinned, bilious with self-satisfaction. I think all of us felt a little broader in the chest behind the arc of the gun.

Bendt's big brain was slow in clicking and that's what took us off guard. The sight of the shotgun took time to register, as did the effrontery of it, and when once the gears began their connections, the gun in our arms completely deranged him. He attacked. He charged us like a horned animal, he charged with steam, he charged with such fury his cohorts froze stiff. Alma screamed.

The shotgun seemed to win a grip on us, Clarissa, Joachim, and me, much like the Ouija board's planchette owns its players, and it ran us toward home and through the back door.

Bendt followed. Into the house.

That took nerve. Joachim and I were stunned. No one had ever broken into our house before. Bendt's intrusion felt as if someone had pulled down our pants. I heard Alma's high pitch. We kept running, and Clarissa, tough soldier, bolting with us into the only room with a lock—the bathroom.

Anchored against the door, the three of us absorbed each shock as Bendt threw the battering ram of his massive shoulder against it, kicked his hooves into it, making uncertain the door's future and our own.

Hours seemed to pass. The powder-blue bathroom had been such a comfort to me. For as far back as I could remember, the blue bathroom was a refuge when chaos trucked in and shook the thing I counted on, this thing I lived in, the physical me. Illness was always somewhat hallucinatory: vomit pouring from me into the blue toilet bowl; crimson nose blood unstoppable and splattering the blue sink; flu pumping the mercury blob; poxes, stings, splinters, and scrapes all remedied with salves, sprays, tinctures, gauze, and bandages from this blue domain. Here was the blue porcelain tub, where Joachim and I dressed in top hats and brassieres of bubbles and we laughed until we knocked ourselves out. Yet in this one swift moment, the powder-blue décor drew a curtain of sadness across my eyes.

"He's going to break it down."

"I'll put a spell on him."

"Oh stop with that! Hold the door, Clarissa." I was on the verge of panic.

Joachim and I clenched the 12-gauge as our sneakers dug into the floor tiles. Clarissa gripped the doorknob. She closed her eyes and mumbo-jumboed something. As terrifying as it was to have him bash at the door, it felt better having

Bendt crash away than not. I know what he might have done had he decided to ransack the house—paw through my dresser, scrawl across my homework, contaminate the fridge. At the thought, a jolt jazzed through my body same as when I plugged my red Snippy Scissors into the hall socket.

The house heaved a sigh and fell silent. It was as if a rainstorm had let up pounding with an abruptness that took even the birds and the worms in the earth by surprise. The three of us conferred, wordlessly, not by exchanging glances but in the exchange of our short and shallow breaths. Was this a trick? An ambush? I opened the bathroom door a crack. I could tell from the light on the landing no one was in the hall.

"Search the house!" I wanted Joachim and Clarissa to scour the entire house, all the closets and under the beds, because I knew I wouldn't sleep unless I had assurance Bendt had departed our home.

"Hello? Hello?" Clarissa's sister Alma stood mid-stairs. "Did you hear? Did you hear?" she whispered with spooky calm. Alma leaned on her sister's magic walking stick, which was shedding bark on our carpeted runner. She wasn't supposed to have taken it from the woods, but under the circumstances, no one complained.

"Make sure Bendt isn't in the house." I was focused on clearing the house of Bendt and his Bendtness. "Get off our property!" I started hollering, half out of my mind, into the air. "Get off our property!"

"Who's she talking to?" Clarissa asked my brother.

"Bendt."

"Bendt? The twins came and got him. They all ran out your back door," freckled Alma screeched. "Bendt peed his pants. He ran right past us. The twins told him the school bus ran over his clarinet and he cried and he peed in his pants and he ran home through the woods. Right past us! Peed in his pants!" Alma slapped her skinny thighs and kept laughing.

Clarissa dropped her end of the gun in exchange for her walking stick. Unprepared, Joachim let the gun bang on the floor.

"Is it loaded?" For the first time all day, Joachim paled.

"No." I didn't know if this was true but I couldn't imagine anyone leaving a loaded shotgun in a cobwebby bedroom corner.

Alma was still cracking up over Bendt blubbering in his sodden wide-wale pants as Clarissa steered her home.

Joachim tried to heft the shotgun. "We have to put it back before mom gets home."

The rare, exciting wail of a police siren bore down on us, increasing our urgency to be done with the gun. Joachim and I watched for a minute through the bay window. A squad car rounded our corner then skidded away, up the hill, where another police car met it from the opposite direction and squealed to a stop. A white Cadillac with a red cross soon followed. All three vehicles pulled up in front of the surgeon's house. The doctor's cronies.

As we struggled to settle the shotgun back in its corner, further damaging the apsara, which would give away our malfeasance, the rescue team was working to beat the breath back into Eugene, who'd just been taken from the rafters in the attic bedroom he shared with two younger brothers. The big world, how grotesquely balanced. At the moment the medics were bringing Eugene down from his martyrdom, his brothers were slipping through our fence, yukking it up at the sight of Bendt mutilated like his clarinet.

Sunshiny Days and Mostly Clear Nights

Laurie Ann Cedilnik
University of Houston, MFA

The virgin on the beach stood chipped and weathered among the rubble. Hurricane coverage called her survival a sign of grace.

The summer before I left for college, my dad split and mom started drinking again and wouldn't stop. On a bad night in June, I stuffed some bras and underwear into a backpack and took the bus to Kennedy, where I called Simone from a payphone. She directed me to take the train to Rockaway, and after an hour of lurching stops, I emerged from underground, surprised I could already smell the ocean.

Simone was waiting in the parking lot near the subway, Jeep engine off, radio on, windows down. She turned to me, smiling, like a talk show host returned from commercial break. "I'm *so* glad you're here."

"Thanks for letting me stay," I said. "I won't be here long."

"Oh, it's fine." She adjusted the rearview. "No one cares."

Even with the windows down, the car's upholstery smelled like weed. Simone had been smoking with her parents since she was fourteen. When I smoked with Simone, I sprayed my clothes with lilac mist and sucked LifeSavers before coming home

The air that rushed into the Jeep as we drove towards the house was warm and thick. When I licked my lips, I tasted salt.

"You can stay in the guest room tonight," Simone said, "but then you'll have to sleep on the trundle in my room. This guy…" She frowned and ashed out the window, paused her radio scan when she landed on Dylan. "Wick's college roommate is staying with us."

Wick was her father, Chadwick Vanderwaal. Way too stuffy a name for Simone's dad. Wick suited him better: thin, tall, sharp. Always lit.

"I can stay someplace else if it's too crowded."

Simone laughed. I wasn't trying to be funny, but I smiled, because if Simone found something funny, I didn't want to admit that I didn't get the joke. For a while, only the DJ spoke. *High seventies this week, with sunshiny days and mostly clear nights. We've got Harry Chapin coming up.*

"Like I said," Simone flicked the butt out the window. "I'm glad you're here."

I had never been to Simone's house on the Point. If Queens is shaped like a Q, Breezy Point is its tail—a thin wisp of land spliced between Jamaica Bay and the vast Atlantic. Simone's parents moved out there each year once school ended. I used to think Wick was a professor full time, but it turned out he only taught one or two philosophy courses a year at the School of Continuing Education. Wick worked like he didn't need the money, and he didn't. He and his wife Alaina would vacate the city in May, leaving Simone in full charge of their Chelsea brownstone. Her dominion over this piece of real estate rendered Simone painfully popular. More painful to me than to her, as I often had to wait in queue to talk with her at school while she was attended by other friends—friends who also lived in Manhattan and had money, friends who glanced right through me because they, like I, couldn't locate what currency there was in my friendship. But Simone and I were starting college in the fall, and so Wick and Alaina had sentenced her to mandatory family time at the Point.

While the Vanderwaal's Chelsea home was crammed with stacks of periodicals and souvenirs of foreign travel, their Breezy Point house felt sparse, almost pure. From the outside, it looked comically traditional—one in a line of squat houses that sat like a row of fat white hens in the patchy crab grass. It had been Simone's maternal grandmother's house, and so it had more of a casual, inviting feel than the properties acquired by the Mayflower-transported Vanderwaals. A few lawns featured flowery grottos whose centerpieces were painted stone statues of the Virgin Mary. Unlike their Catholic neighbors, the Vanderwaals subscribed to no religion.

At the Breezy house, Simone's mother's art dominated the indoor décor. Alaina painted, sketched, sculpted, stippled, glazed. I hadn't seen much of her art until then; it wasn't on display in their Chelsea home. I adored Alaina, but even I could tell her art wasn't very good.

Sim kicked off her Birkenstocks and zeroed in on a cabinet containing a full bar. She poured us two vodka rocks. On a bookshelf, above hardback volumes with gold titles etched onto their spines, stood a sleek brown statue of a nude, faceless woman nursing a baby fox.

Simone caught me looking. "Don't ask." She speared small pickled onions onto silver picks and dropped them into our glasses where they gleamed like pearls.

The vodka burned without a mixer, but I fought against flinching. We were beachside. This wasn't Chelsea, Midori sours at the gay bars lining 23rd Street that never bothered to card. Simone acted pouty when I left the bars, but she was a five-minute walk from home. I was a five-minute walk from the subway, to a short ride and a lengthy late-night transfer, to an epic ride across the length of Queens. So often I'd fallen asleep in a tipsy haze and woken to a kind stranger shaking my shoulder and telling me, "We're here."

I chewed my onion, and Simone told me about a guy at the Roxbury Food Market, a vegan from Ohio who worked the beet stand who she'd been hooking up with. He'd stimulated her with an overripe cucumber.

"I mean *really* ripe," she said. "I came."

She was interrupted by her brother, Connor. ("Named after the Supreme Court justice," Simone told me. "He's lucky they didn't name him Sandra Day.") He raced down the stairs, plucked an onion out of the jar and sucked it like a lozenge.

"Gross," Simone said. Connor popped three more into his mouth and chewed. To see them side-by-side, no one would guess they were related. Simone was tall, with cascades of wild dark hair that she dyed darker still, a blackened blue. A single emerald stud shone in her petite nose, so slight it made her hazel eyes seem huge, even when they were half-shut. Her voice when she spoke was slow, lazy and full of smoke, almost masculine. Connor was short, light, nearly blond, with wide blue eyes that seemed perpetually shocked. His voice was high and he spoke in a rush, as if anticipating an interruption.

"Is that Pam I hear?" Alaina descended the stairs, palms upward as if ready to receive benediction. She wore loose grey linen pants flecked with paint, and a button-down shirt, probably Wick's. Her long French braid was a mess—I spotted a leaf trapped between strands. She enveloped me in a hug, holding me tight, smelling of basil, tobacco, and turpentine. She exhaled into my hair, her breath warming my scalp.

"It'll be okay," she said. "Couples hit bumps. They'll work it out."

I wasn't sure I wanted them to, but I didn't want to hurt her feelings.

"Thanks," I said.

The first two nights in Breezy Point were easy bliss. Simone and I smoked up on the deck, looking out at the bay, then went to the boardwalk for ice cream, buying waffle cones too big for us to finish before a stream of sweet, sticky flavors ran down our wrists.

Wick, with his close-shaved head, thrift store shirts, holey loafers, and Buddy Holly glasses, might have done his best to shake the trappings of his WASP roots, but some traditions remained. After dinner, it was cocktail hour until last man standing. The Vanderwaals certainly drank enough—every night, usually not stopping until the bottle was tapped, sometimes even opening a new one. But the drinking in their family seemed glamorous, whereas in my own home it seemed desperate and sad. Maybe because, at the Vanderwaals, a night of drinking would lead to a spirited discussion on Kierkegaard and Clinton and at home would lead to a spirited discussion on getting *the fuck out of my house, you sorry piece of shit*. I often wondered why my mother couldn't just drink like Alaina, drink until it made her glow instead of glower.

My third night at the house, Connor joined cocktail hour. Sullen, he nursed a can of Budweiser as Alaina, well-past stoned, reflected on his romantic future. "A woman is turned on by a man who she knows *respects* her," she said to him. "You'll see the guys who act like assholes, and you'll see women who worship them and think, 'Should I be an asshole?' You shouldn't. I'm telling you now. Girls outgrow assholes. *Women* outgrow them. They want men who challenge their minds and bodies."

Simone laughed. "Speak for yourself." She passed me the joint. I passed it to Alaina, who appeared not to have heard Simone.

"A relationship *cannot* work if you don't respect a woman's mind."

"Got it," Connor said.

"I'm *serious*. Men don't understand, and that's why there's rape. Can you *conceive*—that we live in a *world*—where men still *rape?*"

"It's fucked up," Connor said, his tone begging, *Please change the subject.*

"It sickens me. I want to know I'm raising our son right. Just promise me that you'll never rape, Connor."

"Jesus! Mom. I'm not going to rape, okay?" Connor's ears flushed red.

Alaina rambled on like a self-absorbed child while her son struggled to rein her in. Wick sat, nodding, bestowing judgment but contributing nothing. It was like being with my own parents.

"How's Connor going to rape anyone?" Simone said. "He's like five foot." Connor's flush spread to his cheeks. He set down his beer and left the room.

Alaina absorbed Simone's slight body in a hug. "Why don't you and Pam go down to the diner, mmm? Mozzarella sticks on me."

Simone stiffened, then shrugged. "Sure." Alaina handed her a bill. "Let's go.

"I never get sent off at night with money when I'm here alone," Simone said when we were out the door. "Should've had you down here days ago."

I smiled, even though I knew it wasn't really a compliment.

I didn't realize until later, but we passed Carter on our way into town. A shirtless man on a blue motorcycle honked at us, and Simone flipped him off. I assumed it was just some perv out cruising, but it was Carter, on his way to her house, trying to say hello.

We didn't go to the diner. Simone lead me to the Slippery Seal, the town's sad pub, where we met up with the beet seller and one of his friends. He draped his arm over Sim's shoulder, his fingers playing at her neckline. I played darts with the friend; I lost. By then, Simone had straddled the beet guy in a corner booth. The friend tried to buy me another drink, but I declined. He put his hand on my bare thigh, below the hem of my skirt, and I let him. I thought about walking back to Simone's house alone, but then there she was behind me, her whiskey breath in my ear.

"We're going to the bathroom to fuck," she said. "Don't leave me."

The friend rubbed my thigh. "Bet you're not like her. You a nice girl? A virgin?"

Was this the best he could do? Maybe Alaina was right—maybe women did outgrow assholes.

"I'm a nice guy," he said.

"Congratulations." The whiskey cokes made me sarcastic. I thought he'd be offended, but the meaner I got, the more he seemed to want to make me like him.

Simone was behind me again. "Not so hot. Better with the cucumber. Let's go."

I worried Alaina or Wick would say something about us being out long past the diner had closed, but when we returned, Wick barely glanced at us, and Alaina wasn't around.

If Wick wasn't talking before, he was talking now. "Let's *hope* Dole gets the nomination," he said to a towering man with a crown of thick of red hair. "Against Clinton? He wouldn't stand a *chance*."

"That's what you'd *like* to believe," The redhead guy built like a lumberjack appeared to be rolling a joint until I noticed the pouch of tobacco. His fingers were thick, but he worked fast, spiraling the paper until he had a thin, neat cigarette that hung from his lips as he talked. "I'd believe that too, growing up with Central Park for a backyard. But that guy, he speaks to a kind of people, people you've never met."

"Come off it, Carter. You act like you grew up slinging steel in Gary."

"I didn't, and I don't pretend to." Their argument faded as Simone poured us water. I followed her upstairs. We met Alaina, legs bare, in Wick's Cornell sweatshirt. Alaina was forty, a year older than my own mother, but she looked a decade younger. Her hair was piled atop her head in a messy bun. She wore glasses I'd never seen, with thick red frames, which made her look younger still.

"Goodnight, girls." She waved dreamily. "I can't keep up with those guys."

"Right," Simone said. "'Night."

The trundle bed that pulled out from Simone's own twin was rigid; I shifted, trying to get comfortable. I could hear the male voices below, rising and falling in argument or agreement.

"What'd you think of Aaron?" Simone asked. I was puzzled, then remembered my prompt disposal of the beet seller's friend's name.

"He's cute." I knew my role—Simone's devoted fan club: her quaint, unhip virgin sidekick. She knew it as well as I did. Too often she'd leave me alone on the Chelsea sofa with a guy she'd hand-picked while she went to her room with her boyfriend, the pothead son of two judges. She'd come to me afterwards, lips puffy and neck splotched, eyes bright with curiosity that dimmed once I disclosed the extent of our cursory gropings. I felt I owed her the hope that someday, soon, I'd become somebody interesting.

Simone yawned. "He *is* cute. I thought you'd like him."

I fell asleep sad. As much as I idolized her, Simone barely knew who I was.

A fairly large part of me wanted to be like Simone: fearless, luminous, free with her favors and herself because she had endless resources. I told myself I was special because, of all her city friends, Simone chose me to be her companion that summer. How easily I forgot that I'd nominated myself.

With no real structure to our time in Breezy Point, days bled into one another. Afternoons were spent on the boardwalk, nights at the Slippery Seal or sometimes, the back deck, Simone in white shorts and loose striped tops that hung off one shoulder and managed to look hotter than any tight, low-cut something I could borrow from her. I'd thought I was being dramatic when I left home without packing clothes, but it was a good ruse. I wanted Simone to dress me. I wanted to don her outfits, like a paper doll, and see if they could make me three-dimensional. I wore her clothes and tried my best to adapt her postures, but underneath, to my disappointment, I was still just me.

As the days passed, I could sense Simone growing annoyed with me. After a late-night couples' retreat to the boardwalk, during which I let Aaron go down on me but was too nervous to return the effort, and Simone and beet guy did God knows what with which vegetables, I laid on the trundle below Simone and we gossiped while her parents and Carter, well into their second bottle of bourbon, laughed and shouted over Manhattans.

"You didn't even offer?"

I stuttered, embarrassed. "Well…I just don't know where he's been, you know."

"If he's experienced, be grateful. He'll know what he's doing."

"I don't want to get, like, herpes."

"Jesus." Simone laughed into her pillow. "Grow up, Pam."

"I'm immature because I don't want herpes?" I was hurt, but kept my tone light.

"You're going to have to start giving guys *some*thing. You can't blue-ball Aaron all summer. Guys won't wait around for a cock tease."

I felt like she had slapped me. I gave her a beat to recover, to say something like, "not that I'm saying you are one," but she didn't. Then I waited for an apology, but that didn't come either. My throat tightened. I was grateful for the dark.

Simone fell asleep soon after that, while I stayed awake and fumed. I heard the clatter of glasses set in the sink, heard the boozy goodnights from Alaina, Wick, and Carter, heard heavy-footed steps on the stairs as the house settled into rest. I slept fitfully, tossing on the trundle. When I woke one time, pre-dawn, I thought the moans were coming from Simone.

At first, I was reminded of someone in pain. But then I listened closer, and heard not pain, but a deep satisfaction, so deep that almost I couldn't identify it as such. I'd never had sex before, and I certainly hadn't made such sounds with Aaron under the boardwalk. Alaina's cries were high and loud. I thought of her doing a kind of ecstatic yoga, her and Wick's willowy forms bending and stretching together.

It wasn't disturbing to hear. It was exciting. And if I couldn't sleep before, I definitely couldn't then. I lay awake, electrified, long after Alaina's last cries.

I woke the next morning with a jolt. I looked at Simone, already up and brushing her hair, an unlit cigarette between her lips. For a moment I felt shy, like last night's eavesdropping had been a shared experience.

"You can sleep in if you want," Simone said. She wasn't being cold, but she also didn't look like she was aching to apologize.

"I'm up."

"Well, I was going to get some sun. Come if you want."

I pulled on a skirt and tank top and followed her downstairs. Carter was in the kitchen, dressed and standing at the counter, eating a piece of pie. Connor sat across from him on a barstool, working on his own slice and a tall glass of milk.

"Morning, girls," Carter said, his mouth full. "Strawberry rhubarb. Want some?"

I did, but Simone said no and then looked at me like I'd better not, either. Just what I needed—a reminder that while Simone's bones fought to jut through her skin, mine were cuddled by an uncharming layer of baby fat. Simone's hair frizzed like a mad genius, while mine just looked mad—a dull, natural brown straw mat that didn't turn heads.

Out on the deck, Simone settled in a lounge chair, pulled her sunglasses down over her eyes, and appeared ready to go back to sleep. She was always so unshakeable, so cool. She never messed up rolling a joint; she was never embarrassed when she tripped, or burped. I wanted to shake her.

"I heard your parents having sex," I said.

Simone lifted her shades and eyed me like I was child requiring her patience. "No, you didn't."

"I didn't? Because I definitely did."

"Pam? You definitely did not."

I was getting to her; I had to be. "I know what I heard, Sim, and I'm positive it was fucking."

Simone sat up. She reached for the mint tin next to her sandals and started rolling a joint. "You're *positive* it was Alaina fucking Wick?"

"Positive. I heard—"

"Yeah awesome, I heard it too. And I'm *positive* it was Alaina fucking Carter."

My face felt hot; I wished for water. She couldn't be serious. Alaina wouldn't do that to Wick, especially not with his close friend. "You think they're having an affair?"

Simone licked the seam of the joint, looked at me like she wished I'd disappear. "It's not an *affair*. Wick knows."

"Knows?"

"It's been going on a long time."

"You're sure? How long?"

"I don't know, but since before high school, at least." *Longer than I've known you*, I would have said. But Simone was *my* Simone—I wasn't hers.

"And Wick, like, doesn't give a shit?"

Simone cupped her hand against the wind to light the joint. "Maybe you haven't noticed, Pam," she began, and humiliation churned in my gut, "but my parents aren't exactly Ward and June Cleaver. *Forsaking all others* sounds nice, but how many people you think actually do it?"

"Wick's not jealous?" If I were him, and my wife was moaning in the early morning with my meaty best friend, I'd cry myself to sleep.

"You think college professors are at a loss for ass? Wake up, Pam."

I thought about the sounds I'd heard last night. I tried to reimagine the scene, switching out Wick's slender body for Carter's broad torso and thick, fast fingers. I expected to feel upset, outraged for Wick or even for Simone, growing up in this family. All I could feel was envy. It was always guys who fooled around while their women stayed home and cried, cutting themselves or burning photos in the bathroom sink. I already thought Simone had everything, but her mother really had everything. Alaina had to be a genius. She had to be the luckiest woman in the world.

But I sensed none of these thoughts would be welcomed by Simone.

"Wow," I said. "That's some crazy shit."

"Tell me about it," she said, and passed the joint.

If Simone was chilly with me in the days after her reveal, I honestly didn't notice. Like a spectator at a crucial match, I was riveted. Wick and Alaina and Carter might not have been the Cleavers but I tuned in religiously, observing every exchange between the trio.

It hadn't been obvious to me. Wick and Carter were the companions, the minds that met and matched. They stayed for hours in the den, locked in loud camaraderie, while Alaina drifted in and out of the room like a cloud. She brought drinks, snacks, stayed a few minutes, seemed bored and left. She and Carter barely looked at one another. How performative was that avoidance: for both of them to stay focused on Wick, to communicate with one another through what they said to him.

Like any devotee to a daytime drama, I had my allegiances. I liked Carter better than Wick. For one, I found him more attractive. He looked, to me, more like what I thought a man should look like: solid, a little extra flesh in the areas you'd press against in a hug, or on a guest bed on a hot July morning. Under the flesh was muscle, which bulged and shifted under his skin when he'd chop wood for the fire pit out back. Whereas Wick often looked as if the giant clay mug of coffee he clutched mornings was enough to topple him.

But Carter seemed to have a soft side that I never saw in Wick. When Connor discovered a dead seagull by the shore and looked like he might cry, Wick didn't try to conceal his annoyance. "Honestly," he said, "it's a *bird*. Save your pathos for human suffering."

That night, on the deck, when Wick went in for the second bottle, Carter leaned in to Connor. "Hey, man," he said. "I think your pathos is righteous." I couldn't help it; my womb seized. I felt sorry for Simone and Connor that he was not their own father. Wick was smug and tacit and took himself too seriously, but I could also tell that that was what Alaina loved about him. She looked at him like he was the thing that made the two of them interesting. His Ivy league philosophy degree, his ancestors who settled New York when it was still New Amsterdam, his aggressive confidence—it enchanted her.

In the week that followed, I saw Alaina and Carter together without Wick only once. I was at the kitchen table making sandwiches for me, Simone, and Connor. Carter poured a bottle of Tanqueray into a glass pitcher. I wanted to start a conversation, but feared an unintended betrayal of what I knew.

Carter broke the silence. "You headed to college?"

"Vassar." I felt acutely aware of my posture, my clothes, how much mustard I put on the sandwiches.

"Big game."

"Thanks."

"You won't be far from Simone." Sim was going to college upstate, too. Some school with no majors, no grades, no one to ever tell you that you were wrong. They also offered (I'd checked) basically no financial aid. "Short drive."

"I won't have a car." Once I said it, I realized that meant Simone would have to visit me. How could I compete with new friends who had the resources to major in nothing?

"Get a Harley." Carter winked at me. It was a friendly wink, not flirtatious. Still, I thought about it that night on the trundle, my cheeks hot, the pulse in my neck throbbing.

"What are you doing!" Alaina burst in from the den. She went up to Carter, slapped him lightly on the hand. "You'll bruise the gin."

"I'll bruise the gin?"

"You have to stir it *gently*—like this." I couldn't see their faces, but I saw their heads bent over the pitcher, heard quiet clinks of ice on glass.

"Is it like bruising fruit? Does it make the gin rotten?" I heard liquid and ice tumble into a glass. "Tastes okay to me."

"Go ahead, make fun."

"You invite it. Look at you, all WASP now, worried about wounding booze." I could hear the smile in his voice.

Alaina bumped her hip against his. "Right. And the Irish are *known* for their flawless rationale."

I had my head bent over tomato slices, but I watched out of the corner of my eye as Carter circled Alaina's bare calf with his large hand. "Wrong," he said, low. "We're crazier than you know."

Alaina brushed his hand away like it was a mosquito and moved towards the cabinets. "Come on, crazy." She took down two more glasses. "Help me carry these." She turned to me for the first time since she'd come in, gesturing with a glass. "You girls want?"

"No, thanks." Sim hated gin.

Carter followed Alaina out, holding the pitcher, one large hand braced against its bottom, like it was something he couldn't afford to break.

When it seemed that the house in Breezy Point couldn't get any more crowded, we learned that Bertha might be headed for New York. The city's coastal areas were warned to board up windows and seek shelter inland where possible. The conversations in the den turned from Montaigne's essays to whether or not the Vanderwaals should head back to Chelsea, and Carter back to Woodside. I waited for someone to address where I might evacuate to, and when Alaina finally said, "You're welcome in Chelsea too, Pam," I was grateful. But Hurricane Bertha is not the storm I remember from the summer of '96.

The Vanderwaals didn't want to evacuate. "Let's wait it out," Wick said, "see how bad it gets," and Alaina agreed.

"If there's a risk," Carter said, "we should just go. Traffic will be murder later."

"But we might not *need* to leave," Alaina said.

Carter kept the radio on, staying alert to updates of the weather. The oldies station played ironic weather-related hits.

"I," claimed one Temptation, "can turn the greyest sky blue," while another bragged, "I can make it rain whenever I want it to."

Then the storm swung closer, and there was nothing we could do but prepare. Simone, Connor, and I gathered up the furniture on the deck and stacked it in a corner of the kitchen. Wick went out for lumber to cover the windows, but when he came back, he realized there were no nails in the house.

"Fuck!" He seemed irrationally angry. "I spent half an hour in that line getting elbowed by teamsters. We don't have any goddamned *nails?*"

"I can head back," Carter offered.

"No, forget it. I'll go. I should have checked."

"I'll go with you," Alaina said. "We should get water, right? And canned stuff?"

"We can get that in Chelsea," Sim said.

Wick smirked. "Is this a storm, or nuclear holocaust?"

No one laughed.

"Just get some water, would you?" Alaina said.

Our amateur carpentry suspended, Sim and I sat outside, legs folded, twin glasses of vodka-somethings sweating on the deck. The weather felt heavy and humid, like rain was coming, but the sky was strangely bright, almost yellow, though with no trace of sunshine. It glowed. It was scary, and beautiful. Through the open kitchen window, we heard a cabinet slam.

"Carter, don't do this." Alaina's voice was even and commanding, like a therapist.

"I love how you can be so calm." I sat up, openly listening. That unshakable calm was the same kind that bothered me in Simone. "Do you *like* being spoken to like you're an idiot Girl Scout?"

"If you're going to be dramatic, we can stop talking."

Sim's jaw was set tight. She reached for the tin and rolled an angry little joint.

"Talk. Bullshit. I get to fuck you and he gets to *talk* to you. He gets to take you home."

"Listen to yourself! Was that not *exactly* what you wanted?"

"Maybe," he said. "Maybe once."

I looked at Sim. She wouldn't meet my eyes. I wanted to say something, but I was too scared to speak. Her hand shook on her matches. She handed the joint over to me, and I did her the kindness of lighting it.

"So what do you want?" Alaina was saying. "You want me to come home with you? Hop on the back of your Harley? That'd get old real fast."

"I'm not Wick. I'm not going to give you half of myself so you can get the other half from somebody else. If you come home with me, be prepared to stay because I will never let you go."

My heart was already going too fast. I shouldn't have taken a hit. But it was the only way I could think to support Sim, who still wouldn't look at me. My own hand shook as I passed back the joint.

"Excuse me? You wouldn't *let* me go?"

"I mean you'll never *want* to go. You'll have to beg me to let you out of my sight. I'm there if you want me." If she said something else, I couldn't hear it. "Try me, Alaina."

I could recognize something frightening in his words, but right then it seemed like the most romantic thing I'd ever heard.

"Carter, come *on*." It was the closest to angry I'd ever heard Alaina. "This isn't a movie. You don't have to ride in on your white horse. I respect you, as a peer. Let's keep this easy."

"Easy for who?" Carter's voice boomed; Sim and I both started. She dropped the joint, stood up, and shot through the kitchen door.

"Shut up," I heard her yell, "you fucking animal."

"Sim," Alaina said, calm again, "it's all right."

"You're obsessed with my family," Sim might as well have been talking to me. "Leave my mother alone."

It was the only time I heard Sim call Alaina *my mother*. I don't know how Carter responded, or what Alaina said next. I ran down the deck stairs, down to the beach, until water lapped at my sandals, and I couldn't hear anything but the shore.

I stayed for hours on the beach. I stayed out after the sun went down and the wind picked up. I shivered in my thin tee, hugging my legs, making myself small on the sand.

When I got back to the house, I was surprised to see Carter's bike still outside. In her room, Sim was asleep, or pretending to be. I lay in the trundle, listening to the wind in the trees. The house was silent.

I heard someone go out on the deck and sat up to look out the window. It was Carter, out for a smoke. My mother's older sister had died young of lung cancer, and I was constantly quitting cigarettes, then bumming a few in order to pose. I was in quitting mode, but I didn't hesitate—I grabbed Sim's Camels and followed him out.

Carter sat in a high-backed wooden chair, facing the water. He looked over when he heard the screen door, and my heart caught to see those searching blue eyes on me. But then his eyes went dark and he turned away, and I realized that he had thought—hoped—that I was Alaina, and was disappointed.

I hadn't remembered to bring out a lighter or even a match, so I took out a cigarette and tapped the filter against my thumbnail. There was a vacant chair next to Carter, but I wasn't brave enough to take it. I saw the crushed remnants of the joint Sim had dropped earlier. I sat on the wood steps, in front of him, as if we were in two separate rows of a theatre watching the same film. The wind had stopped. The night was still.

"Need a light?" he finally asked.

"I guess." I must have sounded like an idiot. I ran through the scene in my head for days afterwards, wondering if Carter knew or guessed why I came outside. I stopped obsessing once I realized that, very likely, he didn't know, and even more likely, he didn't care.

Carter leaned forward and held out his lighter. My hand still shook as I brought the cigarette to my lips, but I inhaled deeply. I took my time thinking of the right thing to say, but he spoke first.

"I'm sorry you heard that."

Back then I thought he was genuinely embarrassed for the scene, but now I realize he probably just wanted to talk about what happened with an impartial audience. I was anything but impartial, but how could he have known?

"That was nothing," I said. "You should see my parents." That was technically true, but also a lie. I had long since grown bored of my parents' fighting, and my father might never come home to fight with Mom again. But Carter's argument with Alaina was fascinating, and fresh as a raw wound. I was willing to betray my own parents' misery for a few moments' conversation. "How long have things—been like this?"

"This bad, you mean?"

Carter raised an eyebrow like, *is this really your business?* but then seemed to reconsider. "Five-some years."

I had so many questions—*How did it start? Was it always okay with Wick? Who made the first move?* —but imaging asking Carter any of those questions felt more shameful than imagining myself stripped on the deck, offering myself as Alaina's substitute. The worst thing he could have done was to leave the porch, cut off our only conversation. In many ways, I feel like the first adult action I took was opening my mouth, and asking.

"Is it always just the two of you?" The rush of nicotine was nothing compared with the adrenaline sparked by asking a relative stranger if he had threesomes.

Carter exhaled. "Christ. Are you kidding?"

"Really, after everything I've heard tonight, you think that sounds so weird?"

Carter laughed and finally looked at me. He shook his head. "Are we that predictable? You know Alaina. Equal opportunity advocate. Ever charitable." He must have seen me trying to visualize the three of them, because he laughed again. "Well Jesus, don't try and *picture* it."

This time, I laughed too. "Why shouldn't I? Nevermind, it *is* weird—are you guys just talking about Nietzsche the whole time?"

"You're a piece of work, Pam." He was still smiling. "No, we talk enough. And that—what you're trying to get at—was a long time ago. I imagine it grows old watching your buddy get your wife off."

I felt my blush deepen. Thank God for the weak, waning moon.

"I heard you two." I said it carefully, so Carter wouldn't mistake my meaning.

"When?"

"Does it matter?"

Carter sighed, crushed the butt under his sole. "No."

He asked if I wanted another smoke; he rolled me my own. I was brave enough to break the ice, and Carter rewarded me with the backstory:

Carter looked up to Wick, always. He was amazed by his ideas and he knew, in his heart, that he was not Wick's intellectual equal. When Wick and Alaina met, Carter was involved in "some ill-advised pursuits," and wasn't around the two much. Later, when he started to turn things around, he sought out the company of his college pal. At first, it had seemed that Wick was the only thing he and Alaina had in common. They tolerated, even annoyed one another, but they were each respectful of the role the other played in Wick's life. Their ideological differences were vast, and that often lent to spirited, tipsy arguments between the two.

"So many times when we'd fight," he said, "we'd end up on the same side of the issue. We weren't so different. I think I saw that first."

Yes, I was eighteen and high on adrenaline and unfiltered cigarettes and I thought Carter was masculinity distilled, so of course I asked: "Are you in love with Alaina?"

"That's the wrong question." His voice took on the disagreement tone, and I reveled in being part of the dispute. He dropped his cigarette into a glass of water; it hissed. He lit another. The smell of the smoke mixed with the scent of wet tobacco. "Love isn't the issue here. I know you're young, and you maybe think you find one person to *love*, and once you've found them, you love them your whole life and that's it—you're done." He took a drag, then another. It seemed that he wasn't going to continue. "If you're lucky, you love one person your whole life. If you're *really* lucky, you love more than one. And if you're me, the one you love the most loves someone else more."

"But that's not a sad story, Pam," he continued. "Because Alaina is not the last woman I'll love. I know that."

"You think Wick's the last man she'll love?"

Carter shrugged. "You got me there." He stamped out his cigarette. "Anyway," he said, clearing his throat and wiping his hands on his jeans, "thanks for listening."

I searched for something else to say, but I was frozen. Carter was already inside before I even thought to say, "No problem." I didn't see him when I went back inside. When I woke up the next morning, he was gone.

I called my mom before we left for the city, to see if she even knew about the hurricane. She cried through the call, promised to get help. In the Jeep, Wick and Alaina made minimal muted small talk beneath the radio music. I sat squished between Sim and a snoring Connor. As we neared the exit for the expressway leading to my neighborhood, Sim turned to me and said quietly, "Maybe it's good if you go home."

"Yeah," I said, though I wasn't ready. "I should." Simone didn't alert her parents, so I thought she might have meant that I should go home eventually. But Wick pulled off at my exit, and I realized they—the family—must have discussed my leaving beforehand.

Sim and I had decent fun in Breezy Point, but after the evacuation, we fell out of touch. Perhaps she sensed my preoccupation with Carter, a preoccupation that, in her mother, obviously bothered her. We both made a show of saying goodbye in the Jeep, citing plans to hang out in the city before we went upstate. But I never contacted her, and she never called me. I never invited her to drive down to Poughkeepsie, and she never offered.

Bertha came and went—it wasn't the big deal the city feared. The Point got knocked around, but no real damage was done. When I heard about the fires from Hurricane Sandy, I studied maps to confirm that the Vanderwaal house was outside the radius of leveled homes. It was. I'm not sure what, exactly, I was hoping had survived.

For months after leaving the house in Breezy, I had intense fantasies about Carter. They were just that—fantasies—and yet they felt like more because I honestly believed that they would someday come to pass. The way some girls honestly believed that they would marry Prince William and become a queen, I was convinced the scenarios I built in my head and rehashed as I rode the train to Poughkeepsie, read European history, touched myself when I was alone—I was convinced that I was just setting the stage, preparing myself for the time when they would finally, physically happen.

I would see Carter on the subway late one night. Before we'd part ways, I'd ask, "What stop is yours?" He'd tell me, then ask, "Want to see my place?" We'd get no further than his couch before his hands would be on me. He'd admire my breasts, say something dreamy about my light pink nipples. He'd push into me and I'd moan, just like Alaina. And then somehow (those steps were always missing), I'd become the next person he loved, the next person he could love more than any other. And as time passed and it became clear that we'd never be lovers, that I'd likely never see Carter again—every year, it felt less and less like a tragedy.

I did see Sim once upstate, my junior year of college. I was at a concert for a band past its prime, whose CDs I'd heard on repeat in Simone's room in Chelsea. The set list reminded me of her, and so when I looked out at the crowd near the stage and saw a girl who resembled Sim, I thought it was a trick of the mind. This girl's face was fuller, her hair short, a natural brown-red color. Her eyes were wide as she swayed to the music, her lids layered in smoky shadow and liner. I had never seen Sim made up. But then she smiled up lazily at a tall guy next to her, and I knew it was Sim. I debated whether to go up to her. For all I knew, she hated me, or thought I hated her. When she crossed to the bar, I saw my chance.

I came up behind her, put my hand on her shoulder. "Sim."

She turned around, and for a second looked blank. I wondered whether I looked unfamiliar, of if she'd just forgotten me. Then her face broke into splinters of sunshine.

"Pam!" She grabbed me in a hug so tight that I laughed out of nervousness.

"You look great," I told her honestly. "It's so good to see you."

"*You* do! Oh my god. I can't believe it, you know?" Simone was pumped full of a boundless energy. I realized she was coked up. "How are you?"

"Good," I said. "Pretty good." What was important to share with Sim?

So, I finally enjoy sex. Maybe too much, if that's possible. Guys I dated looked like they might cry when I suggest opening up our relationship. One of them said, Why don't you just cheat? It's not like I'd know. *One said it was fine, as long as it was with girls, and he could be there or maybe participate, if that was cool. I've stopped dating. It's easier to sleep around. No one yells that way. Nobody cries.*

Or, avoid the topic of me altogether: *Does Alaina still talk to Carter? What about Wick—are they still friends?* But that would be cruel, and I didn't want to hurt Simone. She'd been hurt enough that summer. But as I watched her tap her feet to the rhythm of the bass, I knew that she'd come out of it okay. She'd stayed standing when everything around her had collapsed, and she was here before me, whole.

I smiled at my friend, dumb. I felt so far from her. I was searching for a way to wrap up our exchange when I surprised myself by asking, "How's Connor?"

Simone grabbed my wrist with one hand and let the other hover above her head. "Like a full foot taller than me, you wouldn't believe. *Such* a Romeo. Those Yale girls are all over him."

I smiled. "No way. Little Connor?" My throat was tight and I felt too hot; I wished the bartender would get to us.

"Little panty-dropper. Of course he refuses to make the most of it. He has like, all these moral standards."

"Sounds like him." I tried to imagine slight, sensitive Connor, grown tall as his father but broader, the recipient of damp numbers pressed into his palm at keg parties.

"Wonder if he's still in love with you?"

The bartender had finally reached me. She yelled to ask what I wanted, cupped her ear and waited for my response.

"*Connor*?"

There it was again—that look, the one that said I was a painful naïf—but there was humor in her face this time, instead of spite.

"Pam. Hull*o-oo*. He talked about you endlessly, until Wick made fun of him." For having a crush, I wondered, or for having a crush on me? I let it pass.

"You know," I leaned down, pretending to whisper, "New Haven's really close to Poughkeepsie…."

Sim squealed, pawing my arm like a gleeful kitten. "Jezebel skank!"

The tall guy from before came up behind her and snaked his arm around Simone's shoulder. She bit his wrist. His long bangs were bleached and dyed a faded electric blue. He had two rings through his lower lip. He appeared to be sleepwalking.

"This is my boyfriend."

He held out his hand. "'Sup."

"I'm Pam. We went to high school together." I smiled at Sim with what I hoped was kindness. "She was one of my best friends."

Simone's face contorted in a pained, affectionate pout. "It's so good to see you," she said. "Find us after the show, okay?"

"I will," I said, then gave her a hug, a premature penance for breaking my promise.

The Brackish

Drew Krepp
University of North Carolina Wilmington, MFA

The beach is too clean. Take a handful of sand. Rub it on your skin. Nothing. Sand brushes off. In fact, it gets you cleaner; sand is an excellent exfoliator. Camp on the beach, use sand to scrub your pots. They use sand to form molds for engine blocks because it can be removed so easily. Wet sand can be removed from skin with baby powder.

The beach holds mostly death. Inactive, inert death; very little decay. Clean death. Decrepit sun-bleached shells, their invertebrate souls long gone; gutted and dried crab-shell husks; crisped empty skate cases. An occasional sandpiper, perhaps a stalk-eyed ghost crab, ephemeral as its name, so wispy and light that it looks like it's in your periphery even when in front of you. Maybe a gutted and filleted fish skeleton rots actively, but mostly it's just old, dried death so long gone we treat what's left as things, roll them over in our hands, put them in our pockets, crunch them under our feet. Like they'd never lived, like they'd never engaged their world.

Jenni won't wake up and the baby is not here.

The recovery room is stark and clean, long and narrow with a wide desk facing six or seven beds. Each bed has the same stack of monitors and machines, the same stainless steel stool alongside, the same white curtain on a U-shaped rod overhead. Everything that is not electronic is either white or stainless steel: clean and easily cleaned. It is nothing like the delivery room with the nice wood paneling and comfortable couch, the flat-screen TV, and the wood-framed mirror on wheels so we can "see what's happening," as the nurse said.

The delivery room had been fine until it wasn't. It was waiting and updates, coming and going of nurses and doctors, head under the sheet, head popped out and talking to Jenni, no eye contact with me. Then the day dragged into night and an OB we did not know attached a monitor to my child's brain, sat at the foot of the bed and reached into my wife and inserted the monitor into the soft, unformed part of my unborn son's skull, and when he was done he and Jenni and I stared at the monitor and waited for the beeps. One by one, nurses and technicians came into the room, crowded around its edges, watched the doctor, waited. The beeps came, fast then slow, then stopped for an aching moment, then started again slowly and I noticed that several of the new people in the room had moved closer to me. Something muttered to someone about the fetal heart rate, about it dropping during contractions. Someone handed me a plastic packet of scrubs.

"Put these on. Gather your things but leave them here. Only take your camera."

The operating room was all bright lights and women leading me around by the elbow, calling me "Dad" and moving me around equipment until I was on one side of a vertical sheet with my wife's head, her hair in a mesh net and her hand in mine. People, instruments, sucking vacuum sounds, the rest of my wife's body, and the fetus were somewhere on the other side of the sheet, their spatial arrangement unknown to me. The operating room was people in blue and white, and me, holding on to my seat and to Jenni, a dense burning smell and pointed whispers that I can't quite make out beyond a tone of unemotional urgency. Then someone shows me the baby, just for a moment, swaddled body and gray face, his eyes smeared with clear gel. Then the baby is gone and, hand once more at my elbow, I am led away and Jenni is wheeled into the recovery room.

It is quiet and there is almost no motion at all. The baby is not here and Jenni is not awake and I am listening to my own breathing, concentrating on it because I don't know what will happen if I don't.

Turn your back on the ocean. Walk past the dunes. Pass three rows of houses on stilts, three rows of tacky pun names, narrow shrub-less yards, houses girdled and mounted with bare-wood decks and stairs and porches. Where the tidy mowed grass ends, unkempt saw grass begins, and life ripples through this place. Exposed mud flats move tectonically with the mass micro-migration of fiddler crabs. Minnows gather in a shallow bend of a creek. A heron looms not far away, elegant and lethal in its stalk. Buzz of insects, chirp of birds. Deer trails cut through the reeds. Life meets death here and the seam between the two is the smell, the low strong insistent smell of rot, salt, warmth, damp, earth. Of the life that grows and the death that feeds it.

Jenni can't stop shaking. She's not cold, so says the nurse. It's the anesthesia. The nurse has her head down, writing, and blonde hair falls over her face so I can't read anything from it. This isn't new to her.

The only other occupied bed is the last one in the row, farthest from Jenni's. Also a C-section. She is upright and holding her baby, learning to nurse. Her parents take pictures. Her husband gives her sips of ice water from a Styrofoam cup. All the things the books say you do in the first few hours.

We're not doing any of those things. Jenni had an adverse reaction to her epidural during surgery so they put her under general anesthesia. But it wouldn't matter anyway because our baby is not with us, our little Plexiglas-encased bassinet was discretely wheeled away when they wheeled Jenni into the room. She has not yet seen her child.

The other recovering woman's husband passes me on his way for a refill. He tries to make eye contact, tries to give me a half-smile, some new-dad thing, some unspoken bond we're supposed to share. But I don't want anything to do with him. I don't look at him. I don't know if I'm a dad.

Through the marsh, scramble over the remnants of an old, wooden walkway that lies serpentine, no longer straight, buckled and breached and capsized in the mud and grass. Once it stood over the marsh, now it's in it. A part of it. Arrive at a bluff of land, less than a dozen yards across, no more than a couple feet above water level. A sliver of maritime forest, low-slung scrub oaks, sparse brambles and thorns in the sandy, leaf-littered ground, shady and cool, scattered every so often with deer bones and little starbursts of feathers at bird kill sites. The ocean is now no more than background noise, so low and distant it becomes silence itself. The bluff overlooks a brackish creek, little more than a ditch, sluggish and flat and the blackened-brown of over-steeped tea.

We say "brackish" like its pejorative, impure, like it's not quite this and it's not quite that, like it's some bastardized tertiary outlier. Like brackish is junk water: neither ocean nor potable. But the brackish cherishes balance, embraces complexity, nurtures life while cradling death. Most saltwater creatures cannot survive the fresh, most fresh cannot survive the salt. Those that defy such rigidity find protection in the intolerability of brackish water. Crabs, fish, and reptiles are born and grow and thrive here, safe from the predators that require the salt or the fresh. The brackish gives the small a chance. A chance to enter the world. A chance to kill and be killed, perhaps, but at least a fighting chance.

"Four pounds seven ounces."

That's all the nurse says. She's on the phone with the NICU and I don't even realize that she's talking to me until she hangs up the phone. I look up, she looks at me, neither smiling nor not smiling. I give an awkward nod but I don't know how to react because I honestly don't know whether the news is good or bad and I can't figure out how to ask. She's kind and helpful and young, and seems not yet jaded, and she'd certainly answer my questions but it's 2 AM and I can't form them. Or maybe I don't want to know if my child's life is gasping away in some other undecorated room, a child I've seen for about twenty seconds of his life. A child I've never even held. Four pounds seven ounces. It seems so ungodly small. Too small to support a life. But I don't know.

The nurse returns to her work because this is just another day. I think about how many babies she sees every week, every day. How many powerless fathers she's seen from her desk, who have sat on this stool. I think about how there are so many babies born here that even the dead babies must become routine for these nurses in this clean, clean room. Jenni won't open her eyes and now neither of us can stop shaking.

This is the place. This bank alongside a ruined and now completely collapsed dock at the end of the destroyed walkway, the low branches of the trees not far above me, the water not far below, the miniature forest separating me from the marsh and the little creek, separating me from land, people, intrusion. It is calm here and always quiet, and no one can see me at this place where wood opens to water. I have come here since I was ten, when my parents first bought the house on the opposite bank, just out of sight around a bend. I came to this place on secret nights in my late teens, the house long since sold, driving two hours each way just to sit here for a while where no one knew where I was. I came here for a moment of calm I knew I could not take with me. I come here now, I am hundreds of miles away but I lean into the memory, close my eyes and feel for it as best I can because I remember the calm like I remember the smell and I can't get to my wife and I don't know what has happened to my child, because the light is too bright and the room too clean, because I know now that there will never again be true calm, that with the child comes a vulnerability like nothing I have ever known.

High tide rises steady and without hurry into the creek, doesn't so much as ripple the water as it comes in, the brackish water insensate to the constant death-and-life cycle beneath its impassive surface. The brackish offers serenity, quiet, beauty; blue crabs, mullet, osprey; kayaking, fishing, introspection. The brackish does not offer resolution or answers or better questions. If he lives, I will show him this place I have never shown anyone. But the brackish knows nothing of my child.

Missed

Traci Cox
George Mason University, MFA

The Slovak Internet connection was weak, flickering unsurely as if it might fail at any moment, but the message came through all too clearly. "You need to come home," my father, Perry, informed me over a trans-Atlantic Skype conversation in late January of 2010. "It's time."

When I received the news that my mother was dying and receiving palliative hospice care in our home, I was in Slovakia completing a Fulbright Fellowship. She had been battling stage four colon cancer for four years. I booked a flight home that evening—I'd be leaving the city of Žilina on the last day of February, buying myself a few weeks abroad to tie up loose ends and forfeit my teaching position—and prepared myself for what I might see when I arrived back to Virginia. I knew when I departed for my ten-month teaching appointment in Eastern Europe that I might receive this very call. But distance and time and unfamiliarity of my new surroundings helped me to lose myself and forget what I left behind, and the call—a wake-up call, really—was the beginning of the end for me.

Nothing could have readied me to see my fifty-year-old mother, always made up, always put together, completely changed from how I left her the August before, in 2009. Her heels were replaced with fuzzy bedroom slippers. Her hair, surprisingly still there after months of chemotherapy and radiation, was matted and longer than I'd ever seen it, almost down to her chin, devoid of the usual pomade and hairspray and curls that I was used to. She wore no makeup, and her skin had become yellowed and saggy. She had lost about fifty pounds, and her collarbones jutted out from underneath a purple bathrobe. I imagined putting my hands around them and pulling her up, like a crane. When I hugged her for the first time after seven months of being overseas, I anticipated the smell of Chanel Number 5, but got death instead. Around her hung the odors of urine, and unwashed flesh, and decaying teeth. Some had fallen out, and one of her front teeth had been chipped, a tiny piece, so unobtrusive, so demure, that only someone who had stared at her for twenty-three years would notice.

"It's you, it's you, it's you," she cried as she hugged me. Tightening her thin arms around me, she wouldn't let me go. "I thought you would never come home. I thought you'd want to stay there forever."

"I'm here, I'm here, I'm here," I assured her. "I'm not going anywhere."

The truth is, I didn't want to come home. Abroad, years stretched out before me as they never had before and I envisioned myself teaching English in Bosnia, vacationing on the beaches of Croatia, sliding across the borders of Ukraine and Russia, darting between anonymous concrete jungles, always searching, always adventurous, never looking back. Slovakia had become my new home, and Virginia became a faraway place—not a home anymore, but simply where I was from. Seven months earlier, before seeing my mother hunched at the top of the stairs over a walker, I had watched a tiny animated plane move farther and farther away from my past, across the Atlantic and towards my future, towards opportunity and gesturing to my escape: Slovenkso. Coming back across that same ocean, I felt robbed of the gift I had been given. I wrote only one sentence in my diary on that final day in what had become "my" city of Zilina: "I am grateful, but I am angry." My time would be cut short, and so would my mom's, and nothing seemed fair or right, and would never be.

My dad and I were the primary caretakers of my dying mom, Tina, barely fifty years old at the time she passed away. Hospice workers were scheduled to come and go once or twice a week, but Sarah—a nursing assistant who came to our house quite often—came to be like a member of our family. She had black, almost blue, hair that hung down to her lower back. Sarah had the slightest accent—I never knew where she was from, and I never found time to ask. She smelled of lavender. My mother, a very private and modest person, would not let my dad or I change her colostomy bag, or bathe her, or see her naked. But she let Sarah see all of these things. They talked and talked—about vacations they once took, about Sarah's two young daughters, about jewelry.

My mom told me that Sarah was her best friend. I felt a little jealous—mom and I were always best friends, and I didn't want to be replaced just because I hadn't been home in half a year—but I quickly warmed up to Sarah. She had a soothing way about her, and took her time washing my mother, or changing her clothes, whereas the other hospice nurses seemed to always be in a rush, only concerned with her temperature or pulse.

I arrived home on February 28th, 2010. My mother would only live six weeks longer. During the first week after arriving home, I was struck by how positive she remained. "This is only temporary," she said, her tone apologetic. "I know I don't look very good right now, but I'll get better soon." I remembered a verse from a children's song she sung to me in elementary school whenever something upsetting happened:

Be optimistic
Don't you be a grumpy
When the road gets bumpy
Just smile, smile, smile and be happy.

Around mid-March, my mother began to realize the reality of her situation. She wasn't getting better; she would never get better. About three weeks before she passed away, Sarah came over for her last visit. She was being transferred to a different location and would no longer be able to take care of my mom. Of course, she didn't tell my mom this; she only revealed the truth to my dad and me, to lessen the blow. I think she didn't want to say goodbye to her new friend, either. Sarah, like us, didn't want to see the end.

I heard the scream first, then the sobbing. My mom and Sarah were on the third floor, in the master bathroom, and she was about to wash my mother's hair. I ran up two flights of stairs and stormed into the bathroom, fearing the worse: bleeding, a fall, or immense, unbearable pain from somewhere deep and unreachable inside.

My mother was crumpled on the floor, crying. Sarah's hands rested gently on the tops of her shoulders in a gesture of comfort.

"What happened?" I demanded to know. "Why is she so upset? I've never seen her like this before."

"Your mom looked in the mirror," Sarah told me with a face that uncharacteristically displayed worry and sadness. "I told her not to, but she did anyway. She—well, she didn't like what she saw."

"I'm a skeleton, I'm dying, I'm ugly," my mother gasped out between sobs. "I look terrible, I look terrible," she repeated. I didn't know what to say. Sarah assured her that everything would be all right, but I knew it wouldn't. She did look terrible—skeletal, sickly. Standing there, naked, in front of that mirror, she stared at death, and it stared back. And death wasn't temporary.

I did the only thing I could think of. I wanted to make it better, to make her pain go away, to cover up and hide the state of her wasting body. I grabbed a few cosmetics from her plastic makeup organizer near the sink and had my mom stand, her right hip leaning on the porcelain counter for support. Sarah placed her arm around my mother's waist. First, I applied mineral foundation in swirling motions to her yellow, dry skin, covering up any discoloration or hyperpigmentation near her nose and mouth. Dipping two fingers into a dusty rose-colored cream blush, I gently patted the rouge onto her cheekbones, emphasizing the highest points, as she had once shown me years ago. It was difficult to put mascara on her wet, teary lashes, but a shimmery golden shadow made her eyes look less puffy. Lastly, I applied lip gloss—her favorite shade, a sheer red with flecks of gold—and told her to look in the mirror again.

"Not too shabby," she said. I grabbed a peach-colored loose-fitting silk tunic shirt from her closet—it still had its tags—and draped it over her thin, wobbly frame. "Oh, that's a nice color," she noted, examining herself in the mirror. "I thought I'd never get the chance to wear this shirt." She wasn't really smiling, but at least she had stopped crying.

"Remember when you taught me to do my makeup, Mom?" I asked her. She nodded in response. "That's definitely something I inherited from you: an obsession with makeup." I remembered the times we used to go to Sephora and Ulta together and spend hundreds of dollars between us on high-end cosmetics, but quickly stopped myself. I realized then that we'd never shop for makeup, or clothes, or groceries, together again.

"I taught you everything you know," she said, looking me dead in the eye. "No matter what happens, I'll always be with you. You hear me?"

It was my turn to nod, so I did, holding back tears. I couldn't let my mother see me cry, it would only upset her more. So I waited an hour until she fell asleep in the living room, and rushed to my bedroom. I'm not sure how long I lay in bed, face down, screaming into my pillow, but I know I lost my voice for the rest of the day.

My mom saw me in heaven in a red silk dress. She told me about this vision two weeks before she died. When she woke up from her fitful, groaning sleep, she liked to tell me her dreams. I'd sit on the side of her hospital bed, positioned in our living room cockeye to the television set, and she'd hold one of my hands cradled in both of hers. Along with her dreams she often had vivid hallucinations during the last two months of her life as she lay and waited to die of colon cancer, disoriented and muddled with oxycontin and dilaudid and ketamine and a mélange of other drugs that pulsed through her bloodstream at all hours of the day. In heaven, although all alone, she said I was happy, that I had never been happier, in this red dress. I smiled in heaven, and twirled around, showing off the folds and contours of my outfit to anyone who would watch, as I might have done as a little girl.

"You look so good in red, but you don't wear it often," she told me, the long fingernail of her first finger tapping my shoulder for emphasis. The last French manicure she would ever have was chipped; the slightest traces of white paint still remained on the tips of her nails. She wore one of my dad's old XXL bleach-stained t-shirts, cut completely up the back from seam to collar so that she didn't have to pull it over her head. "You look good in color."

"I don't like to wear red, Mom," I reminded her. "It's too bright for me."

Tightening her grip on my hand, she looked up at me. "You were alone, in heaven. But I don't want to be alone. Will you be there waiting for me?"

"I have to stay here, Mom," I told her. "You go. You get everything ready for us, and we'll follow you soon, and I'll wear a red dress so you'll know it's me."

"And a flower in your hair?" she asked me, childlike, excited.

"I'll wear a flower if you want me to," I told her. "I'll wear a red rose."

And then, loosing the grip on my hand, she smacked my wrist. "Well, *duh*. You still have to match your *outfits* in heaven."

Of all her recounted visions, however, this is the only pleasant one I can recall. The others are riddled with fear and anxiety and pre-terminal agitation. She wasn't really my mother anymore; her mind was someplace else, someplace dark, unable to remember our names, oftentimes mistaking me for a nurse. At night, she would watch as mice ran across the floor towards her. In reality, what she saw were balled up socks, unmoving, unthreatening to someone with a clearer head, a brain that wasn't being eaten away by disease. We couldn't see what she did. Occasionally, household items were imagined out of their scale in my mother's eyes. My father placed a small wooden organizer on the kitchen counter for bills and mail. She looked at it one day and asked how the building across the street went up so quickly. The builders were nowhere to be found, so how did it happen without her noticing? She's always looking out of the windows, she said. She knows our townhome community in Ashburn, Virginia, "better than anybody." Apparently the neighbors took down their fences, and the heating pad was a cardboard moving box, and the bedspread hatched red-eyed baby mosquitoes. At night I could hear the scratching of her chipped, gel nails on the floral comforter.

Two days before she passed away, my dad and I decided to move her out of our living room and into a hospice care facility. We could not administer the high doses of medicine she needed in our home. She went insane in our house, showing signs of aggression and delusion a week before she died. We could not control her from physically harming herself and lashing out at us. Sometimes she screamed so loud that I thought our neighbors would call the cops. On her final morning in our home, she ripped out the IV from her upper arm, took off her robe, and rolled out of her hospital bed. She couldn't walk, and didn't get far, but that didn't stop her from shouting. "You're trying to kill me!" she yelled. "You promised you wouldn't do this!" My dad and I were promised by nurses and doctors that she would die peacefully, quietly, in her sleep—no pain.

We'd have time to say our goodbyes. But I didn't get the chance to say goodbye to my mom. None of us—not my dad, not my mom, not me—wanted to see what we were seeing, real or imaginary.

But we did see. "It's difficult to see the beginnings of things, and harder to see the ends." Joan Didion wrote that, and when I saw my mother cold and unmoving on a hospital bed at the Hospice House thirty minutes after she passed these few words came to mind. But all I could see was the end. It wasn't hard to. The end was lying right in front of me, in a blue and green floral nightgown that did not belong to my mother. The end had its eyes closed and the red, chapped fingers of both hands interlaced and resting on a swollen, hardened belly. The end felt like sunken temples when I brushed the back of my hand against her head, and the end had its warmth sucked out with its last breath. The end was not nigh, but here, and I wondered how I would begin again.

When the end was happening, I was in my car, driving to see her. At 9:29 a.m. on Tuesday, April 20th, I received a phone call that informed me my mother had just died. That's how the caller from Hospice House said it: "I'm sorry to tell you this, but your mother just died." Not passed away, or was gone, or was no longer with us; she had simply died, alone, and unexpectedly. The caller's wording was deliberate, and to the point. A month before I was asked by another hospice nurse if I was "ready for the big show," and I wondered what kind of person—what kind of caregiver—would say something like that.

"She had a fever early this morning and was having trouble breathing. And then…she died." *And then…and then?*

I was the one to know first. And I didn't make it in time. I took the news in stride, hung up my cell phone and made a decision to keep moving on, keep moving forward in my silver Honda CR-V, the car that had belonged to my mother for eleven years before I inherited it at age twenty-three when she could no longer drive. I looked up at the SUV's cloth ceiling and saw grey stains from her cigarette smoke. She would not hold a Virginia Slims Ultra Light again.

Half an hour after receiving the news, I arrived at the small, neat brick building, its manicured lawn welcoming, not telling of the events that transpired each day inside its walls. I saw her there on a cot, yellow and unmoving, in what they called the meditation room at Hospice House, although it felt like that room gave you no room to think, it was so crowded with other people's memories and death and mourning.

A nurse wearing a freshly starched lab coat greeted me with a cold, ungloved hand. She smelled of hand sanitizer and disinfectant. I recognized her voice immediately from the phone; I'll never forget that voice, although her name escapes me now.

"Would you like to see your mother?" she asked me. Another strange question, as though my mom was simply waiting for me in the next room, enjoying a diet Dr. Pepper or a coffee, lighting a fresh cigarette. She would scoot over on the hospital bed and I'd lie next to her and we'd catch up after not talking for a few days. I'd comment on the drabness of the decorations, and she'd elaborate on how much she hated the fake waxy flower arrangements placed in every corner.

"Yes, I would, please. Thank you," was all I could say in response. My father, also too late, was silent.

The nurse stood next to me as I examined my mother like a person might examine a statue or a painting in a museum. Detached, critical, taking it all in. It was not my mom, but a body, a shell, empty.

"Your mother is very thin," she commented. I agreed. I noticed her protruding cheekbones, her sunken eye sockets. Someone had brushed her hair.

A minute passed. "If she looked anything like you in life, she must have been very beautiful," the nurse said. I smiled at the unusual compliment and opened my wallet to display the last professional photo of my mother, taken three years prior. She sits against a blue background, her hair recently cut, thin pink lips turned slightly up at the camera. My dad sits behind her in the photo. I wondered if it was their last photo together, if he knew as he stared at the lens that things were about to change forever. They were married for 25 years, and he still swears he'll never marry again.

"She could have been a model," the nurse remarked, nodding in appreciation at the photograph, and I told her that at one time, she was, in her early twenties. She never went to college, but in her mid-thirties attended nursing school to become an LPN. Tina-wina, as my dad used to call her, maintained her good looks until she became too ill to apply makeup or do her hair. I wanted to remember my mother that way—her lipsticked half-smile, her arched and shaped eyebrows. But my admiring memories of her had been replaced with the duties of taking care of a dying human—instead of painting each other's nails, I cleaned her bedsores while she cried, humiliated. We didn't watch television together but I watched her every day, observing with fixed concentration her chest laboriously rise and fall and rise, dreading the moment when it would fail to ever rise again. I began using her Chanel perfume and sprayed her bed linens and robes with Febreeze.

The finality of it gets to me. No more miracles; she really wished for that. "I'm waiting for my miracle—I've waited four years, so it's coming soon," she'd tell the hospice workers, just a few weeks before she died. We wished for it, too, until the day my mother passed, and a different kind of miracle happened. She was at peace, even though those she left behind were not. And the realization of the events gives us no mercy, no hope. Just emptiness in the house; quiet. When I moved back home after graduating from James Madison University, I used to walk into our family home around midnight on a Friday or Saturday night, slightly tipsy from an evening out with friends, and while slipping off my shoes in the foyer I could hear the din of the television upstairs. It was a constant in my home, the flickering images, the chattering of voices from the plasma screen. My mom had always been a night owl, and stayed up late watching reruns of *I Love Lucy* and *MASH* and ordering jewelry and makeup off of the Home Shopping Network or QVC. She'd greet me, ask me if I'd like some coffee, or tea, or would I like to see the new bracelet or jacket she just ordered? And usually I'd sit for a minute or two, recounting events of the day—how was work, I put up a new birdfeeder on the deck, tomorrow we have a radiation or chemo or blood work appointment—nothing deep, or profoundly special, or life-affirming.

"I missed you at home tonight," she'd say. "My Traci."

It's these little moments I miss the most. I come home now after a long day or night and the house is dark. My dad's working late, or driving around, or watching a lacrosse game somewhere. The television is off. The couch goes unoccupied. Smells of coffee and tea are nonexistent, and no one is home to ask me about my day.

CPSIA information can be obtained at www.ICGtesting.com
Printed in the USA
BVOW01s0700240913

331786BV00004B/22/P

9 780985 340711